Tuna Does Vegas

by
Jaston Williams   Joe Sears   Ed Howard

A Samuel French Acting Edition

MUSIC USE NOTE

Licensees are solely responsible for obtaining formal written permission from copyright owners to use copyrighted music in the performance of this play and are strongly cautioned to do so. If no such permission is obtained by the licensee, then the licensee must use only original music that the licensee owns and controls. Licensees are solely responsible and liable for all music clearances and shall indemnify the copyright owners of the play and their licensing agent, Samuel French, Inc., against any costs, expenses, losses and liabilities arising from the use of music by licensees.

IMPORTANT BILLING AND CREDIT
REQUIREMENTS

All producers of *TUNA DOES VEGAS must* give credit to the Author of the Play in all programs distributed in connection with performances of the Play, and in all instances in which the title of the Play appears for the purposes of advertising, publicizing or otherwise exploiting the Play and/ or a production. The name of the Author *must* appear on a separate line on which no other name appears, immediately following the title and *must* appear in size of type not less than fifty percent of the size of the title type.

TUNA DOES VEGAS had its world premiere at the 1894 Grand Opera House in Galveston, Texas, on August 4, 2007. The performance was directed by Ed Howard, with sets by Christopher McCollum, costumes by Linda Fisher, lighting by David Nancarrow, and sound by Ken Huncovsky. The production stage manager was Ken Huncovsky. All roles were played by Joe Sears and Jaston Williams.

CHARACTERS

Traditionally, in the plays set in Tuna, Texas, the characters are all portrayed by two actors wearing costumes rigged for quick changes and miming most hand props excluding costume props like purses and canes. The plays can also be done with up to as many actors as there are characters and with as many properties as desired.

When all characters are played by two actors, one actor plays:

THURTON WHEELIS – A radio disc jockey

BERTHA BUMILLER – A middle-aged housewife

AUNT PEARL BURRAS – An elderly chicken farmer

LEONARD CHILDERS – Radio station owner

INITA GOODWIN – A waitress

JOE BOB LIPSEY – A community theatre director

SHOT – A hotel security guard

ELVIS 11 – An Elvis impersonator

When all characters are played by two actors, the other actor plays:

ARLES STRUVIE – A radio disc jockey

DIDI SNAVELY – A used weapons store owner and **MAMA** - her mother

PETEY FISK – Head of the Tuna Humane Society

CHARLENE BUMILLER PUGH – Bertha's pregnant daughter

VERA CARP – Head of Tuna society

HELEN BEDD – A waitress

ANNA CONDA – A hotel proprietress

MAURICE – A hair stylist

WO-HU – An acupuncturist

ELVIS 42 – An Elvis impersonator

SETTING

ACT I
TUNA, TEXAS
Scene 1: Radio Station OKKK – Early one Morning
Scene 2: Bertha and Arles' Home – Later that Morning
Scene 3: The Tastee Kreme – That Evening
Scene 4: On a Plane to Vegas – That Night

ACT II
LAS VEGAS, NEVADA
Scene 1: The Parking Lot of the Hula Chateaux – Two Days Later –
Valentine's Day – Early Morning
Scene 2: Inside the Hula Chateaux – Later that Morning
Scene 3: The Hotel Lobby – Later that Afternoon
Scene 4: The Undertow Cabaret – That Evening
Scene 5: Back Home in Tuna – That Night

ACT I

Scene I, 1:
Radio Station OKKK – Early One Morning

VOICE OF ARLES. *(radio V.O.)* This is Radio Station OKKK in Tuna, Texas, serving the greater Tuna area at 275 watts, signing on.

(Lights pop up on **THURSTON WHEELIS** *and* **ARLES STRUVIE.***)*

THURSTON. Good morning Tuna, this is Thurston Wheelis.

ARLES. And this is Arles Struvie.

THURSTON. And this is the Wheelis…

ARLES. Struvie report.

THURSTON. And first off in the news, the local chapter of the Smut Snatchers of the New Order has canceled all meetings until further notice according to Vera Carp, who serves as acting president any time the Reverend Spikes is under indictment or in rehab. It seems the Smut Snatchers have become a victim of their own success.

ARLES. They have.

THURSTON. They have.

ARLES. They have. They have.

THURSTON. Yep, after banning the complete works of just about everybody, having declared Leviticus required reading in Biology and removing various words from the dictionary, there just doesn't seem to be anything left to ban.

ARLES. I don't think they got rid of a library book since they went after BLACK BEAUTY.

THURSTON. What's wrong with BLACK BEAUTY?

ARLES. Vera says that it is chock full of subliminal images.

THURSTON. Oh yeah. What is a subliminal image anyway?

ARLES. I don't know, but this is Texas, and we won't put up with them. We won't.

THURSTON. We won't.

ARLES. We won't, we won't.

THURSTON. Vera urged all members to remain vigilant and keep seeking spiritual guidance and points out that two years ago when they thought they'd banned all possibly offensive words, in a two day period they came up with poot, pecker and boob. So, if you know of any words that Vera might find offensive, pick up the phone and call 'em in to her. She'll appreciate it.

ARLES. She will.

THURSTON. She will.

ARLES. She will. She will. Well, folks, if you don't have anything better to do, make a call down to the Tuna Little Theatre and try to cheer up Joe Bob Lipsey. The theatre's artistic director has been in a creative slump since the poor reception for his musical version of *Gone with the Wind* titled *Something Blowing in Dixie,* which the local critic labeled a complete waste of crinolines. Friends are voicing concern, and they say that Joe Bob locks himself away for hours listening to the soundtrack of "Funny Lady" over and over, and that he is experimenting with fad dieting again.

THURSTON. What one is he on this time?

ARLES. I think it's the Rush Limbaugh diet.

THURSTON. Is that the one where you only eat what you can spell?

ARLES. That's it. You know, I saw Rush last year at a broadcasters' convention, and hell, I'll tell you one thing, he sure knows how to spell butter.

THURSTON. Just awful.

ARLES. So folks, if you've got a minute, give 'ol Joe Bob a call.

THURSTON. Ship him some fettuccini.

ARLES. He'll eat it. He will.

THURSTON. He will.

ARLES. He will. He will. Thurston, how about that weather?

THURSTON. Well folks, our weatherman Harold Dean Latimer hasn't shown up today, which means he's probably out chasing tornadoes and sometimes they chase him right back, but he called in his forecast, and it says minus rain, hail, or a dust storm, we can expect it to be sunny.

ARLES. And folks, speaking of sunny, I'm going to be off the air for a few days while my dearest baby Bertha and I head to Las Vegas to work on our tans and renew our wedding vows on Valentine's Day.

THURSTON. It looks like once would be enough.

ARLES. It does.

THURSTON. It does.

ARLES. It does. It does.

THURSTON. What are you going to see while you're there?

ARLES. Well, I want to see that old boy that fires those dwarfs out of that giant slingshot, but this is Bertha's vacation. I'm just going to follow her around and pray she'll back out of going to the Liberace Museum. But, I want you to know that while we're in Las Vegas, we're going to think about all you folks here in Tuna. We will.

THURSTON. They will.

ARLES. We will. We will. We'll think about y'all about once ever forty-eight hours. *(He laughs.)* But folks, stay tuned.

THURSTON. Stay tuned.

ARLES. Coming up next we've got our ever popular "He Done Her Wrong Monday Morning" show, where you'll hear twenty classic country cheating songs in just under two hours. But right now, we have a word from our sponsor, Didi Snavely of Didi's Used Weapons….Wait a minute. I've got a message here. Thank you, Ronny. This just in from our State News desk: "Former Texas Representative pleads insanity, checks into mental hospital. Says he wants to spend more time with his family." That's touching. It is.

THURSTON. It is.

ARLES. It is. It is.

THURSTON. I get all emotional.

ARLES. Please, hold it together.

THURSTON. This is Thurston Wheelis…

ARLES. and Arles Struvie…

THURSTON. with the Wheelis –

ARLES. Struvie Report.

(Fiddle music. **ARLES** *exits and changes to* **DIDI**. **THUR-STON** *exits and changes to* **BERTHA**. **DIDI** *enters.)*

DIDI. This is Didi Snavely of Didi's Used Weapons asking you, are you tired of wasting time and money on anti-depressants and expensive doctor visits? Well, come by the store and elevate your mood the cheap and easy way with a good old used weapon from Didi's. For that low-life burglar sneaking in an unlocked window, how about our petite, mother-of-pearl, inlaid snub nose? I call it the Sweet Sue; it's compact, decorative and deadly through double pane glass. Or if it's animals you're after, our Bambi Maker sure-shot deer rifle is perfect for most large game and the occasional drunk, belligerent hunter. Buy two, and we'll throw in that gun rack for half price. So come by the store, scratch that itchy trigger finger, and remember what we always say at Didi's, "Don't just hang up on telemarketers, track 'em down and shoot 'em."

*(***DIDI*** exits and changes into ***ARLES***.)*

Scene I, 2:
Bertha and Arles' Home – Late Morning

(Patsy Cline music plays as **BERTHA BUMILLER** *enters, moves to kitchen counter, pours coffee, and turns off the radio.*** **ARLES** *enters carrying his boots, sees* **BERTHA**, *and sneaks up behind her.)*

ARLES. *(grabbing* **BERTHA** *from behind)* Gotcha!

BERTHA. Ahhhhh!!! Arles, you scared me. Lord, what will the neighbors think hearing me scream like that?

ARLES. Well, they better think fast, 'cause we'll be outta town by noon, and they'll be left to snoop on each other.

BERTHA. Still, I don't want them hearing me scream like a banshee.

ARLES. That's why you're gonna like Las Vegas. Why, there's a strange sound coming behind every closed door, and nobody even bats an eye.

BERTHA. Really? Even on Sundays?

ARLES. Yep.

BERTHA. Well, I just hope we're doing the right thing spending all this money renewing our wedding vows.

ARLES. Well, we can't back out now. I'll never get the deposit back.

BERTHA. And I feel all strange not having any bridesmaids or family.

ARLES. Oh, they got a bridesmaid on call. They throw her in for an extra fifty.

BERTHA. Damn, that's a lot of money.

ARLES. You're worth it, Baby, every nickel. Just think, this time tomorrow you'll be slopping on suntan lotion by the pool at the Hula Chateaux Resort.

BERTHA. Oh, Arles, I can't be traipsing around the hotel in a swimsuit. Somebody might see me.

ARLES. Baby, we don't know a soul in Las Vegas. What do you care if somebody sees you?

---

*See Music Use Note on Page 3.

BERTHA. Well, I get all shy. I suppose you're right. Why should I worry about what some stranger from Nebraska thinks about me no matter how sophisticated they might be, and Pearl gave me her floral swimsuit. She said she was too big to go swimming. She claimed boats tried to tie up to her.

ARLES. Your Aunt Pearl is funny as a crutch.

BERTHA. Arles, go look in my closet and see if you can find my good suitcase.

(**ARLES** *exits and changes to* **PETEY**.)

ARLES. Is that the one you won in the Lion's Club raffle?

BERTHA. Yes. This will be the first time I've used it for anything but funerals. It will be great not to have to pack that black pantsuit in it. Oh Arles, I'm so excited about going to Las Vegas. We haven't taken a real vacation since the last time we went to the prison rodeo. That's why I chose Vegas. I love the prison rodeo, but I want to go on vacation to a place where I don't know everybody.

ARLES. *(off)* I couldn't agree more.

(The doorbell rings.)

BERTHA. I'll get that. You dig out that suitcase.

(**BERTHA** *gets the door.* **PETEY** *enters.*)

PETEY. Hi, Bertha.

BERTHA. Hi, Petey. I don't want another animal; so don't ask.

PETEY. I'm not here by about a pet placement, I just came by to see if Jody would keep an eye on the animals at the Humane Society while I'm out of town.

BERTHA. I'll have him call you. Where are you off to?

PETEY. Las Vegas.

BERTHA. Oh. When?

PETEY. Today.

BERTHA. Why?

PETEY. Well, I was listening to Arles on the radio and realized it would be a great place to conduct an investigation concerning surgical animal tampering as well as exploitation of show animals. Plus there are a significantly high number of white jungle cats in that town. I intend to find out if they're true albinos or just victims of bad dye jobs. I mean it's tough enough to be all white in animal society where there is a clear prejudice to stripes, spots and pigmentation, but to take their claws away on top of it just adds insult to injury if you ask me.

BERTHA. Petey, how old was your mama when she had you?

PETEY. I think I resent that remark.

BERTHA. Well, how do you plan to get close enough to those animals to check them out?

PETEY. Oh, connections are everything. My cousin is a skin diver in Las Vegas.

BERTHA. Petey, Las Vegas is in the middle of the desert.

PETEY. I know that. Carlton is a skin diver in one of those big hotel fountains, unclogging the pipes. You can't imagine what people throw in there.

BERTHA. I don't want to know. Please, don't tell me. I'll have Jody call you.

PETEY. I appreciate it, Bertha. See you in Las Vegas.

(**PETEY** *exits and changes to* **ARLES.***)*

BERTHA. Oh yeah. *(to herself)* Oh God. *(calls off)* Arles, did you find my suitcase?

ARLES. *(off)* Is it the brown one with all the bumps on it?

BERTHA. That's fake ostrich skin.

ARLES. *(off)* It's beyond me why anyone would want luggage that looks like it's got the chickenpox.

BERTHA. Oh, it's very fashionable.

(**ARLES** *enters.*)

ARLES. It's up on that top shelf. I'll need this chair to get to it. *(He starts to exit with a chair.)* Who was that at the door?

BERTHA. Petey Fisk.

ARLES. I pray to almighty God you said no.

BERTHA. It's not about pawning off another animal; he's decided to go to Las Vegas.

ARLES. Why?

BERTHA. He's got a cousin there who's a skin diver, and they're going to make sure those big jungle cats still have their claws.

ARLES. I guess I'm supposed to understand that.

(**ARLES** *exits with chair and changes to* **CHARLENE.**)

BERTHA. Petey wants all the cats in America to keep their claws.

ARLES. *(off)* Baby, Hell. Have you seen the teeth on some of those big cats? The fangs? Hell, if you ask me, claws are overkill.

BERTHA. Well, I don't think I'll be taking that swimsuit after all.

ARLES. *(off)* You sure as hell are. Baby, Petey's the one person in town who won't talk. Besides, he doesn't notice anything that comes without feathers and a tail.

BERTHA. You're right about that. You know how shy I am; have been for years. It got so bad when I was a teenager; I had to shower in the dark

(*The phone rings.*)

BERTHA. I'll get that.

(*Enter* **CHARLENE BUMILLER** *on the phone. She is visibly pregnant, holding a baby, with another, older baby slung on her back papoose style, and a toddler dummy Velcroed to her leg.*)

Hello.

CHARLENE. Mother, you didn't send that money in regular mail; did you?

BERTHA. What's wrong with regular mail?

CHARLENE. Oh, nothing that doesn't involve me herding these kids into a truck and standing in line with 'em at the post office.

BERTHA. Well, send Rayford.

CHARLENE. He's down in his back.

BERTHA. Again?

CHARLENE. Don't take that tone. He can't even go bowling. Everybody who's had back trouble says it's some pain.

BERTHA. That's some back.

CHARLENE. I wouldn't expect any human kindness from you, running off to Las Vegas while I'm pregnant like this.

BERTHA. Charlene, if we waited for a time you weren't pregnant, we'd never get out of the driveway. And I'll have you know we're staying in our second choice hotel just so I could send you and bad back the extra money.

CHARLENE. Oh, let me see if I can remember the lyrics to "Cry Me a River."

BERTHA. Does Rayford have any job prospects?

CHARLENE. He can hardly work when he's flat on his back.

BERTHA. I've never seen him work standing up.

CHARLENE. That's class. Mock the sick. Rayford lives in pain; he's barely able to move.

BERTHA. Charlene, he's had you pregnant since he's known you. How does that happen if he can't move?

CHARLENE. Well, I don't have to listen to this. Have fun gambling away my inheritance and tell Arles I hope sending us the money didn't cut into his liquor budget.

BERTHA. Honey, the first time I see you when you're not pregnant, I'm going to slap the snot out of you.

(The baby poops. **CHARLENE** *smells it; makes a face.)*

CHARLENE. Well, y'all have fun. Don't think twice about me. If I feel contractions, I'll just drive myself to the hospital.

BERTHA. Well, Charlene, on the way, you might want to swing by the drug store and pick up some rubbers.

CHARLENE. Ohhhhh!!! My own mother saying rubber! Gag a maggot. I gotta go.

(**CHARLENE** *hangs up, exits and changes to* **ARLES**.)

BERTHA. I swear to God, she makes me so damn mad ringing me up every time she runs out of bean dip. Lord, she ate so many Cheetos when she was pregnant with little Thurman, I swear that kid had an orange tint to him. Arles, honey, while you're in there would you dig out my makeup bag. I think it's under the bed.

ARLES. *(off)* O.K. Sure thing Baby.

(We hear the sound of a dog barking wildly, **ARLES** *as* *HOP-SING.)*

Damn it, Bertha, he's at it again.

BERTHA. Oh Lord, Hop-sing. Hop-sing! Cut it out right now. You pushy little Pug. I told you the next time you turned on Arles, I was goin to Napoleon your butt to the backyard. Get out there and snap at that Chow if you have the nerve.

*(***BERTHA*** lets the dog out.* **ARLES** *enters with luggage, puts it down.)*

ARLES. I'm trying to remember why we have that dog.

BERTHA. Petey Fisk.

ARLES. Oh yeah.

BERTHA. I'm sorry about Hop-sing, Arles.

ARLES. Baby, this is getting out of hand. I can't get near your side of the bed without him snapping at my ass.

BERTHA. Chinese Pugs are funny that way. You know that.

ARLES. I bet that's why they eat 'em over there.

BERTHA. Stop it.

ARLES. Kinda makes me want to look up a recipe.

BERTHA. I mean it.

ARLES. Who was that on the phone?

BERTHA. Charlene.

ARLES. Asking for money.

BERTHA. I already sent it.

ARLES. Don't tell me. It's his back again.

BERTHA. Bingo.

ARLES. My back would hurt too if I never got out of bed.

BERTHA. She claims he's looking for work.

(**BERTHA** *exits and changes to* **PEARL.**)

ARLES. Rayford's too lazy to own a self-winding watch. The only way he'll ever bring home a paycheck is if they all end up on Jerry Springer.

BERTHA. *(off)* Please to God, don't even mention it. Well I'm going to dig out that makeup bag.

(**ARLES** *moves to the refrigerator and opens it.*)

ARLES. Baby, do we have any of that Tahiti Punch left?

(**ARLES** *makes a cocktail, all the time keeping an eye on the bedroom*)

BERTHA. *(off)* I think there's a can behind the buttermilk dressing, but, Arles, don't you be mixing a drink. I want you to wait till we get on the plane.

ARLES. All I want is a little punch to wash the dust down my throat.

BERTHA. *(off)* Uh huh.

ARLES. Have I ever told you, you need to work on your suspicious side? You really do. You know what that is? That's a character flaw. It'll age you before your time. I'd hate to see that happen. I would.

(*The doorbell rings.*)

I'll get it.

(**PEARL** *enters.*)

Hello, Pearl. Come on in.

PEARL. Arles, thank God I caught you before you got away.

ARLES. What's up, Pearl?

PEARL. What time is your flight leaving for Las Vegas?

ARLES. We're heading out of Lubbock at six o'clock tonight.

PEARL. I'll meet you at the airport.

ARLES. Why?

PEARL. Oh, I have to go with you.

ARLES. What makes you say a crazy thing like that?

PEARL. You'll think crazy if I miss that wedding. Why it could jinx the whole marriage.

ARLES. It' a little too late for that, Pearl; we're just renewing our wedding vows, besides you missed the last one. We eloped, remember?

PEARL. And when you came home you had that rabid squirrel living in your fireplace.

ARLES. Oh hell yeah. What a mess. He got so hungry, he tried to eat Bertha's wax fruit.

PEARL. I gave her that banana. It had been in the family for years.

ARLES. Well Pearl, that's just one example.

PEARL. Oh no, I missed my cousin Emerdee's wedding 'cause she married a man from California. There was a taboo against that at the time.

ARLES. Is she the one with the hair thing?

PEARL. Oh, yes her hairline started at her temple and petered out two inches later.

ARLES. I met her, and her best hair was growing out her ears.

PEARL. Oh, she should've combed that over. Well, she went ahead and married that gunsel from California, and one year later they had triplets that looked like her and had his brains. I'll never forgive myself.

ARLES. One of those triplets went to prison.

PEARL. Oh, it gets worse. Of the other two, one's a lawyer and the other's in Congress.

ARLES. Well, you never know how your kids are gonna turn out.

PEARL. Don't tempt fate. I missed another cousin's wedding. It was her second. She was old. Older than you. Birth control never crossed her mind. Four short weeks later, she was pregnant as a church mouse.

ARLES. She couldn't have been that old.

PEARL. Oh, she was stuffing envelopes for A.A.R.P. when the doctor called. Of course, I can stay here if you think I'll be in the way.

ARLES. Hell no. I may not be retirement age, but I'm too damn old to start playing peep-eye. See you at the air-port, Pearl.

PEARL. Goodbye.

ARLES. God Almighty

(PEARL *exits and changes to* LEONARD.)

BERTHA. *(off)* Well, I found it.

(ARLES *starts making another drink, one eye on the bed-room.*)

ARLES. Found what?

BERTHA. *(off)* That makeup bag. Now if I can just remember where I hid that swimsuit. Who was that at the door?

ARLES. Pearl.

BERTHA. *(off)* What did Aunt Pearl want?

ARLES. She's going with us to Las Vegas.

BERTHA. *(off)* She what?

ARLES. She says you could get pregnant if she doesn't go.

BERTHA. *(off)* Are you making this up?

ARLES. I'm just relaying information. Don't act surprised. She's your family.

BERTHA. *(off)* Well, I'm not taking that swimsuit.

ARLES. Calm down, Baby. Pearl's family. Besides, that old woman's eyes are so bad, she can't see beyond her knuckles. Keep looking.

BERTHA. *(off)* Well, I guess.

(*The phone rings.* ARLES *answers it.*)

ARLES. Hello.

(LEONARD CHILDERS *enters on the phone.*)

LEONARD. Arles, Leonard. I'm so Goddamned mad at you. It's got me chewing on Motrin.

ARLES. What the hell have I done to get you all haired up, Leonard?

LEONARD. Flapping your jaws on the air about you and your Valentine baby going to Vegas to renew your vows has got my wife all nutty. She's just booked us to Vegas and bought tickets to hear some foreign screaming Mimi caterwaul about caresses and body heat and corners of the night. Makes me want to projectile vomit. I haven't seen Reba this hot and bothered since Inglebert What's-his-dink recorded "The Way We Goddamned Were."

ARLES. It can't be that bad, Leonard.

LEONARD. The hell it can't. I just saw her packing a lavender nightgown and two dozen batteries into a suitcase. God only knows what the hell she's up to.

ARLES. Leonard where's your sense of romance?

LEONARD. It's right next to my twenty-twenty vision. In case you've forgotten my wife is a wilderness scout. Twenty-five years of chasing things through cactus and brambles and jagged rocks does terrible things to a body. I damn sure don't want to look at that in a short lavender nightgown.

ARLES. I take it by your tone you don't intend to renew your wedding vows.

LEONARD. Only if I can ask the preacher what the hell I was thinking the first time. I ought to fire your ass.

ARLES. By God, go right ahead. Let's see you have to work for a living. I'm your top rated show, seventy listeners and up, but if that's not good enough for you, then fire me, and I'll pack up my Patsy Cline albums and go.

LEONARD. Oh hell, you wouldn't take Patsy.

ARLES. *(Adding a shot to cocktail.)* And you can try reading the news crammed in that little, tiny room with Thurston wearing enough Hai Karate cologne to gas a rat.

LEONARD. Now there's no need to get emotional here.

ARLES. Kiss my ass, Leonard. Thurston's been dying for a shot to play disco records. I'm the only thing that stops him. Let's see how much fertilizer you'll sell when those farm boys wake up to *(He sings in falsetto.)* "Oooo, love ya, love ya, Baby."

LEONARD. I didn't mean to imply that I was really going to fire you.

ARLES. Shut up, Leonard. You've always been all steak and no potatoes, but you need to remember how things work here in America. You may be the owner, but if I don't show up and work, your privileged ass will starve. You got that?

LEONARD. Oh hell yes.

ARLES. And while I've got you, make sure you get to the airport a little early. We got tons of luggage and we could use a hand. Don't be tardy.

LEONARD. Oh hell no.

ARLES. Bye, Leonard.

LEONARD. I'm leaving right now.

*(**LEONARD** hangs up, exits and changes to **BERTHA**. **ARLES** turns on the radio to catch the end of a song, sits to put on his boots.)*

THURSTON. *(over radio)* Ahh…. Well, that was Miss Patsy Cline. Thank you, Patsy. Well as you know, it's our policy to play some Patsy Cline every hour on the hour, but since Arles and Leonard are on their way to Las Vegas and I'm in charge of the play list, let's just flash back to the Seventies with that signature smash "Boogie Oogie Oogie."

*(Music: disco hit)**

ARLES. Oh hell, it's already started.

*(**ARLES** turns off the radio.)*

BERTHA. *(off)* Why are you playing that music?

ARLES. It's the radio station. Blame Thurston.

---

*See Music Use Note on Page 3.

BERTHA. *(off)* Lord, I thought my brother Denver was back on a visit.

ARLES. Gahhhh!!! Your little brother Denver is the only person I know who brings his own music at Christmas time.

*(***BERTHA*** *enters with more luggage, puts it down, takes* ***ARLES****' drink from him and pours it down the sink.)*

BERTHA. It soothes his nerves. He's such a big city person. Every time he gets out of Amarillo, he gets all anxious.

ARLES. When he comes to Tuna, I get all anxious.

BERTHA. Be nice. He's a good boy, and he's done real well with his lampshade business. He holds the local record for selling the most track lighting.

ARLES. Well, I'd hate to think of Amarillo in bad light. Well, I'm going to run across the street to the Snacky-Pac, get some Burma Shave and some throwaway razors. You need anything for the trip?

BERTHA. I can't think of anything.

ARLES. I'll be back in a jiffy.

*(***ARLES*** *exits and changes to* ***DIDI****.* ***BERTHA*** *moves to the door, calls out.)*

BERTHA. Arles, I forgot, pick me up a pair of tweezers and some of that wild cherry-flavored Chap Stick if you don't mind.

ARLES. *(off)* Sure thing, Baby.

BERTHA. You need any money?

ARLES. *(off)* Nah, I got it covered.

(The phone rings. ***BERTHA*** *picks up.)*

BERTHA. Hello.

*(***DIDI*** *enters, on the phone.)*

DIDI. Pickles.

BERTHA. Hello, Didi.

DIDI. Pickles, I've got a bone to pick with your husband. Mama heard him going off about Las Vegas on the radio, and it sent her from bad to worse.

BERTHA. How so?

DIDI. Well, you know I've had her playing imaginary Bingo for years. It's the only way to control her. Well, now she's got Las Vegas on the mind, and she switched to imaginary roulette. Hang on. I'm going to give her something to calm her down.

(She pours from an imaginary kettle into an imaginary cup.)

I have to go in her room. She's so deaf; she can't hear a mule fart.

(as she exits)

Mama.... Mama, Lookie! Here's some hot Dr. Pepper with lemon and sugar, just like you like it.

MAMA. *(off)* Red, thirty-nine. Bet it all. The baby needs shoes. Well spin that son of a bitch!

*(**DIDI** re-enters.)*

DIDI. Can you hear her going off?

BERTHA. She sounds pretty worked up. What are you going to do?

DIDI. We're leaving tonight for Las Vegas.

BERTHA. Oh good.

DIDI. I'm going to park her crazy butt in front of a Keno board and feed her half a dozen baby aspirin; I'm going to the gun show.

BERTHA. And where are you going to be staying?

DIDI. Some place called the Hula Chateaux. We got a hell of a good deal.

BERTHA. What a coincidence.

DIDI. I checked out some of those bigger resorts, but I wouldn't sleep a wink in one of those places that looks like Rome or Egypt or France. You know why those empires fell, don't you?

BERTHA. Why?

DIDI. They didn't have any guns.

BERTHA. Didi, the French have guns.

DIDI. Yeah, but they're too busy sautéing or groping each other to get to 'em. If you want to conquer France, all you got to do is attack during lunch. But I checked out that resort and it says they have a high diving board, which is wonderful so I can work on my cannon ball. *(She looks off.)* Oh Mama, God…damn it! Aw, I gotta go. She's tangled in the blinds again.

*(**DIDI** hangs up and exits, changes to **VERA**.)*

BERTHA. Bye, Didi. I swear, when Arles gets home, I'm gonna suggest we just stay here and rent the movie.

(We hear Hop-sing dorking a squeaky toy off stage.)

Oh Lord, he's at it again. Hop-sing! Hop-sing, stop dorking that plastic duck right now. Petey didn't tell us you were a sex maniac. Stop it. All I need is for one of the Smut Snatchers to drive by and see you doing that. Lord, a call from Vera Carp would send me straight to shock treatment.

*(The phone rings. **BERTHA** picks up. Enter **VERA CARP**, on the phone.)*

Hello.

VERA. Bertha

BERTHA. Vera.

VERA. Bertha. Bertha. Thank the Lord you're there. I'm as moody as Liz Taylor at Wal-Mart with this Smut Snatchers situation. If we don't find something to ban in the next couple of weeks, we could lose our national certification.

BERTHA. Vera, I'm real busy.

VERA. Well, I'm sorry, but we've been friends all these years, and I'm teetering on the verge of a depression.

BERTHA. Well, take a pill, Vera.

VERA. Narcotics are never the answer. Did Moses take dope when he wandered in that desert for forty years?

BERTHA. I doubt it.

VERA. Granted he should have started out with a map, but he didn't start popping Valium. And did Daniel smuggle goofballs into the lions' den?

BERTHA. Not to my knowledge.

VERA. Did Mary scream for narcotics when she gave birth in that stable?

BERTHA. Well, she would have if she could have gotten her hands on some. You need to distract yourself, Vera. Get your mind off your problems.

VERA. I've done all the things that usually work. I fired the maid.

BERTHA. Why?

VERA. She was too short to dust the top shelves. I warned her about it. Every time I came into the room, there she was standing there, being short; they don't want to be any better. And I finally broke down and sent Virgil back to military school.

BERTHA. I thought he hated that place.

VERA. That's the point. I had no choice. It was the third time I caught him lip synching "Dream Girls" in my hair curlers. Something had to be done.

BERTHA. Well, if he keeps getting in your hair curlers, maybe he wants to be a beautician.

VERA. If that day ever comes, make sure the mortician doesn't lay me out in coral colored lipstick. I'm counting on you. But back to the Smut Snatchers, I still think we should consider banning the word finger when it's used as a verb.

BERTHA. Vera, we've been through this before. You start talking parts of speech to the Smut Snatchers, it puts them all to sleep.

VERA. Well, we'll just have to get down on our knees and pray till something nasty comes up. Speaking of which, if you're really serious about going to that filthy Las Vegas, I hope you're packing rubber gloves for the trip.

BERTHA. I'm sure we'll be fine.

VERA. You'll find lots of stuff that needs banning there, I suppose. Wait a minute. That's it. The Lord works in mysterious ways. If we're looking for smut and sin and potty talk, that's where we'll find it. I'm going with you.

BERTHA. Oh Vera.

VERA. It's no trouble. I'll protect you from all those moderates. Why with me there, it will be like you never left home. Hang on. Virgil, you take my bubble bath back to my bathroom… now. I gotta go search his luggage. Last time we sent him to military school, he smuggled in my best brazier. I gotta go. See you in Gomorra.

BERTHA. Bye.

(**BERTHA** *and* **VERA** *hang up.* **VERA** *exits and changes to* **ARLES**.)

Lord, I swear, there's not going to be enough people left in town to run a stop sign. Makes me so damn mad. All I wanted was five days, just five days, maybe once every ten years, of not having to come up with three meals a day, every day, day in and day out, and having to clean up, sweep up after everybody. Five days away from the friends, family and loved ones, who are about to drive me to a spot on the post office walls. Who's going to call next? Geraldo?

(**ARLES** *enters.*)

ARLES. Baby, they were out of wild cherry, so I got sour apple instead.

(**BERTHA** *sits and starts to cry.*)

All right, into the bathroom right now.

BERTHA. What?

ARLES. When you start crying over Chap Stick, I know you haven't been taking your hormones.

BERTHA. It's not the Chap Stick. Vera just called. She's going to Las Vegas.

ARLES. Why?

BERTHA. She's looking for more things to ban and boycott.

ARLES. She ought to boycott those white shoes. Big old feet. You can see them from Jupiter.

BERTHA. Stop it.

(**BERTHA** *laughs.*)

ARLES. Don't worry about Vera. She isn't going to stay anywhere we like. She's too good for the Hula Chateaux.

BERTHA. But she'll drive us nuts on the phone.

ARLES. I'll yank that sucker out of the wall.

BERTHA. Oh Arles, you're so manly. But I'm not going to risk being seen in that swimsuit.

ARLES. Baby, we're going to get that swimsuit wet if I have to spread a tarp out in the hotel room and go at you with a squirt gun.

BERTHA. That's nasty.

ARLES. Come on, Baby, we're going to the Liberace museum.

BERTHA. Oh, you changed your mind.

ARLES. I'll buy you all the shrimp scampi you can wolf down.

BERTHA. You know I love shrimp scampi.

ARLES. We'll knock back Mai Tais and save those little umbrellas.

BERTHA. For my collection.

ARLES. Come on now. Baby, just think, five whole days in a place where you can have Venice without the pigeons, New York without the Yankees, and Paris without the French, how good can it get?

BERTHA. All right. Grab those bags and give me the keys. I'll drive.

ARLES. Why?

BERTHA. 'Cause you're drunk.

ARLES. Oh yeah.

BERTHA. Happy Valentines!

(**ARLES** *picks up the luggage and they exit.* **BERTHA** *changes to* **INITA,** *and* **ARLES** *changes to* **HELEN.** *Music: disco tune)*

Scene I, 3:
The Tastee Kreme – That Evening

THURSTON. (*on radio*) This is Thurston Wheelis, and if you're like me, you've had enough of the mainstream media trying to regulate everything from greenhouse gases to marsh mellow cream. So, join me a week from Saturday for the Javelina Club's monthly Break-Your-Diet Pork-Out Night, where every covered dish is required to contain simple carbohydrates, preservatives, bacon grease, multiple dairy products, and/or processed cheese food. So, leave the high-fiber raw broccoli and roughage for those who don't know MSG from Shinola, and fill up on food that makes you feel like a real American. All proceeds will go to help defray expenses for Javalina Club member Juanelle Rainey's second quadruple bypass operation. And folks, for the two of you who have been calling in all morning asking for more country favorites, all I can say is you'd better learn to live with your disappointment, 'cause it's time to get down and boogie!

(*Music: a disco dance tune.* HELEN *and* INITA *enter as music blares on the radio.*)

INITA. Turn that up.

HELEN. I'm in Hell. (HELEN *turns off radio.*) This disco has been going on for four solid hours. I've never gone that long without country music.

INITA. Oh, come on Helen, this music takes me back to the 70's. (INITA *turns radio back on.*) Think of all those great memories.

HELEN. I remember all the penicillin shots we had to get. I'd rather not be reminded. (HELEN *turns off radio.*) I'd call Thurston and try to get him to play something else, but he won't talk to either of us. He still claims you tried to poison him.

INITA. That wasn't my fault. That was a bad can of beans, and he knows it.

(**INITA** *turns radio back on.*)

HELEN. Girl, the only people you're fooling with this disco nostalgia are the one's who've already left town. (**HELEN** *turns off radio.*) Everybody knows you're trying not to think about that cowboy.

INITA. I don't know what you're talking about.

HELEN. Donnie Spurburg.

INITA. What about him? (**INITA** *turns radio back on.*)

HELEN. He's the reason you swore off cowboys again after he left you wrapped in a shower curtain at the Super Budget Motel. (**HELEN** *turns off radio.*)

INITA. You swore you'd never bring that up.

HELEN. Well, I'm about to crack. All our good customers are in Las Vegas except Joe Bob. Vernon says we could close down a few days but Joe Bob's thirty percent of our business, so it's no way, José, and they're having that big rodeo in Las Vegas right now.

INITA. *(trying to stay carefree)* I don't care. (**INITA** *turns radio back on.*)

HELEN. I know you, girl. (**HELEN** *turns off radio.*) Once you get your fill of this disco crap, you're going to crater. I'll find you back there weeping in the pickles. You know you're bi-polar.

INITA. That's a lie. I've never touched another woman in my life.

(**INITA** *turns radio back on.*)

HELEN. And to make things worse, Joe Bob's still on that Rush Limbaugh diet. I'm not that good at spelling either.

INITA. Next time Joe Bob comes in, I'm gonna hand him a bowl of M & M's and tell him to choke on them.

HELEN. You two need to smoke a peace pipe.

INITA. Don't say smoke. I'm trying to quit. I may get the patch.

HELEN. Garland had a patch; said it didn't work. He couldn't keep it lit.

(*They both laugh.*)

I love Garland, but he's got the brain of a prairie dog.

(**HELEN** *turns off radio for the last time.*)

INITA. It doesn't take brains to do what he does.

HELEN. I heard that.

INITA. Helen, we need to change the subject to something besides cowboys.

HELEN. There's hundreds of 'em waiting in Vegas.

INITA. And I've gotta stay here and grill patties for Joe Bob Lipsey.

HELEN. Speaking of the devil, he's pulling up right now.

INITA. I'll be in the kitchen. When you two start spelling, I feel like I'm back in Mrs. Barch's fourth grade class.

HELEN. I liked Mrs. Barch.

INITA. Well you were a Baptist. She had it in for the Pentecostals. I'm outta here.

(**INITA** *exits and changes to* **JOE BOB**. **HELEN** *picks up the phone and dials.*)

HELEN. Well, all I can do is try. Hi, Thurston, it's Helen. Don't hang up, please. No. No. I wouldn't dream of complaining, but I was just wondering if maybe you could play something a little more country for old time's sake. Well, I don't know, but couldn't you at least play some Linda Ronstadt from that period in the 70's when she lied and claimed to be a country singer? Well please come up with something, at least for me.... I had nothing to do with that bad can of beans. No, No, every time we have a lawsuit they take the papers directly to the kitchen. Okay, what have you got?... Dolly Parton's disco period? Well, thanks but no thanks. No, Dolly affects Inita's dental work, and I'm not wild about that quaver in her voice. It always sounds like she is having car trouble.... Don't get huffy with me. I know a loose fan belt when I hear one. I've gotta go.

(**HELEN** *hangs up. Enter* **JOE BOB LIPSEY,** *the local theatre director.*)

JOE BOB. Helen. Quick. *(he spells)* Dr. P-E-P-P-E-R. Quick. Quick. I have to hydrate. This diet is killing me.

HELEN. Do you want your ice *(she spells)* S-H-A-V-E-D or C-U-B-E-D?

JOE BOB. Both.

HELEN. Excuse me.

JOE BOB. B-O-T-H!!! Are you happy?

HELEN. You made me promise to stick by the rules. Now how else may I help you?

JOE BOB. I want a B-U-R-G-E-R with P-I-C-K-L-E-S and O-N-I-O-N-S.

HELEN. Do you want your O-N-I-O-N-S G-R-I-L-L-E-D?

JOE BOB. Of course

HELEN. Anything else?

JOE BOB. Fries.

HELEN. Excuse me.

JOE BOB. F-R-Y-S

HELEN. Oh Joe Bob I am so sorry! It's F-R-I-E-S.

JOE BOB. You're kidding.

HELEN. *(showing him a menu)* No. Look.

JOE BOB. This is Hell. Oh, well. A bag of C-H-I-P-S.

HELEN. What kind of bun?

JOE BOB. Sesame.

HELEN. Spell.

JOE BOB. Alright. I have to stay calm. *(He spells slowly as if in a spelling bee.)*
S-E-S-A-M *(long pause)* -E.

HELEN. *(jumps for joy)* Yeah!

JOE BOB. Thank Christ.

HELEN. Do you want your burger dressed?

JOE BOB. Just catsup.

HELEN. Uh-huh.

JOE BOB. K-E-T-C-H-U-P.

HELEN. Oh Joe Bob I'm sorry. It's C-A-T-S-U-P.

JOE BOB. Both spellings are acceptable.

HELEN. Not according to Mrs. Barch.

JOE BOB. God, that old bitch made the fourth grade hell and she is still at it.

HELEN. I liked Mrs. Barch.

(**HELEN** *takes the order to the kitchen.*)

JOE BOB. You were a Baptist. She had it in for boys who wore sandals.

HELEN. *(off)* Inita feels the same way about Mrs. Barch. Ya'll have that in common.

JOE BOB. I can assure you, I have nothing common enough to connect me with Inita Goodwin and I'll waltz right into that kitchen and tell that to her face.

(**HELEN** *returns.*)

HELEN. That's a bad idea Joe Bob. Remember what happened the last time you did that?

JOE BOB. No, what?

HELEN. She kicked your ass.

JOE BOB. Oh, yeah.

HELEN. Besides, you need to be nice to Inita. She's had a real bad day.

JOE BOB. Oh, did they discontinue Henna #44?

HELEN. I'll have you know Inita's hair color is natural. It says so on the package.

JOE BOB. Oh, yeah. Right. Tell her to shake the bottle next time.

HELEN. Oh, please. What do you know about hair? Besides, like I said, you two have a lot in common.

JOE BOB. Like what?

HELEN. You both hate Vera Carp.

JOE BOB. Oh, Yeah.

HELEN. You both love to eat.

JOE BOB. At least I use a fork.

HELEN. You both have trouble spelling.

JOE BOB. That's Mrs. Barch's fault.

HELEN. You're both afraid to fly.

JOE BOB. I blame that on that airplane movie where Karen Black landed that jet. I can't relax knowing there may be a slightly cross-eyed flight attendant in the cockpit.

HELEN. Inita's worse. Every takeoff and landing she runs down the aisle screaming "We're all going to die!" They got her profiled. She can't even get through security. You two need to declare a truce. All we've got the next few days is each other and that disco garbage that's on the radio. I'd kill to be in Vegas with everybody else.

JOE BOB. There's irony for you. Every rube in this town is taking in the bright lights of Las Vegas and here am I, the only one who can truly appreciate that town, the man who brought showmanship to Tuna, the town that wasn't ready for an all-female production of "Of Mice and Men". Never do theatre in a town that's a four letter word, and I have to sit it out here tempting ptomaine.

HELEN. Stop being dramatic. That hasn't happened in months. *(She suddenly gasps.)* Wait a minute! Joe Bob, are you serious about wanting to go to Las Vegas?

JOE BOB. Of course I am. Why?

HELEN. I can make it happen. We have to drive, but there'll be the three of us. We can take turns.

JOE BOB. Three?

HELEN. You, me and Inita.

JOE BOB. Have you checked the pilot lights around here? It sounded like you said you, me and Inita.

HELEN. Well, yeah.

JOE BOB. I'm not traveling cross-country in a car with her. I don't have time to get my shots. The first thing she'll do is take off those greasy cook shoes, and the smell will cake our teeth.

HELEN. She'll keep her shoes on; I promise. And one of you two can always be asleep in the back seat while the other is up front with me. This way we can all go.

JOE BOB. No, Helen. I can't see it. I'll just stay here and eat.

HELEN. Well good. You can be the guinea pig for our new menu.

JOE BOB. New menu?

HELEN. We'll have linguini parmesan.

JOE BOB. I can't spell that.

HELEN. And lasagna pomeranio.

JOE BOB. Oh Jesus.

HELEN. Enchiladas del Consuelo.

JOE BOB. You know Helen, you sometimes can be a real B-I-T-C-H. You know that?

HELEN. And sushi.

JOE BOB. I can spell that.

HELEN. And we'll give you all the raw catfish you can eat.

JOE BOB. AHHH! O.K. When do we leave?

HELEN. I'll be right over with your B-U-R-G-E-R and C-H-I-P-S.

JOE BOB. *(as he exits)* I've gotta run home and get my show tune collection.

(**JOE BOB** *exits and changes to* **INITA.**)

HELEN. Okay, one down, two to go. *(She dials the phone.)* Hi. Vernon.... No, nothing's wrong with the new grill.... Nobody's threatening to sue. I just wanted to let you know we're going to close the restaurant for a few days and go up to Las Vegas. Joe Bob's going with us.... No, Vernon, I don't make business decisions, but I do know your wife Nancele's cell number and I also know how I got groped every time you're in the restaurant.... Groped. G-R-O-P-E-D. Oh, God. Joe Bob's got me spelling everything.... Of course I'll tell her.... I know she's handy with a gun. I used to shoot skeet with her. Bye, Vernon. You enjoy Midland.... Oh, I know you will. Bye Vernon. *(hangs up phone)* Inita get in here! Girl, we're going to Las Vegas!

(**INITA** *enters.* **HELEN** *starts closing down.*)

INITA. Don't tease me, Helen. My heart won't take it.

HELEN. I'm for real, girl. I just called Vernon. We're closing down the restaurant for a few days. There's only one catch.

INITA. What?

HELEN. Joe Bob's going with us.

INITA. Helen, you can be a real bitch when you want to be.

HELEN. Why does everybody keep saying that? I'm just trying to make everybody happy.

INITA. Oh, I'll be real happy trapped in a car with that. You know how I hate a man with an earring. Ever time I see it, I want to rip it out and grab him round the neck and squeeze till it pops his head off.

HELEN. Don't hold that in girl; it could fester and turn into something really bitter.

INITA. I'm still not over "Oklahoma."

HELEN. That wasn't fair. He should have cast you as Ado Annie.

INITA. I was born to sing "I'm just a girl who can't say no," and he gave it to Connie Carp.

HELEN. I know. She's just a girl you hope says no. But Inita, don't you see, there's no other way. Joe Bob has to go, or Vernon won't let us close. We've got a pact that one of you two has to be asleep in the back seat at all times. You won't even know he's there.

INITA. Well…

HELEN. Think, girl; thousands of cowboys. Thousands of 'em.

INITA. Alright, I'll do it. But he sings one show tune, and I'll pound his head with a high heel.

HELEN. Oh yeah, that's another point. He won't go if you take your shoes off.

INITA. Is he spreading rumors about my feet stinking again?

HELEN. Girl…you need to face up to that. After you stand all day in the greasy kitchen, your feet smell like Port Arthur.

(**HELEN** *goes into kitchen to get Joe Bob's order.*)

INITA. All right, but if he so much as hums 'I feel pretty', he'll arrive in Vegas with butterfly bandages. And I mean it.

(**HELEN** *re-enters.*)

HELEN. That sounds fair. I've got his order, shut off the grill. I'll flip the sign and we're on the road.

INITA. Oh, Helen, all those cowboys. Do you think Donnie Spurburg will be there?

HELEN. I thought you were finished with him.

INITA. Says who?

HELEN. Said you, after he left you passed out on that fertilizer tank.

INITA. You swore to God you wouldn't bring that up again. At least he never torched the trailer.

HELEN. Cletus was just trying to be romantic, he's a little dyslexic, and he misread the instructions on that butane candle. Now, you get in the backseat. You need to be asleep by the time we get to Joe Bob's.

(**HELEN** *exits and changes to* **VERA**. **INITA** *exits and changes to* **PEARL**.)

Scene I, 4:
On a Plane to Vegas – That Night

VOICE OF CARLOTTA. Good evening Ladies and gentlemen, I'm your flight attendant Carlotta, and I want to welcome you to BUDGET BIRD *(static)*, stand by our motto "We'll get you there one way or another." *(static)* …you folks are on our direct flight to Las Vegas, with intermediate stops in Yuma, Flagstaff, Lake Havasau City…. *(static)* …if we reach our desired cruising altitude, which can be a little iffy…. *(static)* …equipment failure, oxygen masks are supposed to fall…. *(static)* …before helping them with theirs. *(static)* …with watered down drinks…. *(static)* all correct change *(static)* … Thank you. *(static)* …with us.

(Lights come up on **PEARL** *entering and sitting on a plane during above. Enter* **VERA**, *who crams her bags into overhead compartment.)*

VERA. Well hello, Pearl.

PEARL. Oh my God Vera, what are you doing here?

VERA. Well, first class was full, the only empty seat was here in the no class section next to you. Isn't fate funny?

PEARL. I don't hear anybody laughing. *(pushes her flight attendant call button)*

VERA. The only hotel available was some dump called the Hula Chateaux, thank the Lord I got the penthouse.

PEARL. Oh, God.

VERA. Now, calm down, Pearl. I'll be glad to get your oxygen mask on you. It's my Christian duty.

PEARL. Keep your hands away from my face. I need your help like a hog needs a sidesaddle.

*(***VERA** *crosses in front of* **PEARL** *to sit.)*

VERA. Of course, you do. I wouldn't let anything happen to you. You're like the 100-pound gourd at the County Fair. We're all just so amazed that you even exist.

PEARL. Oh, I'd rather ride strapped to the wing. *(pushes her flight attendant call button)*

VERA. Ooo…wouldn't that be a pretty sight. Now, if you need anything, let me know, and I'll go fetch it.

PEARL. Does that mean if I say fetch, you'll run off?

VERA. Well, we don't want you making any sudden moves. The weight shift could doom us all. Personally, I'm a little concerned, considering our sinful destination.

PEARL. Oh, I can't wait to hit the crap tables.

VERA. Shh…God is listening.

PEARL. Don't shh me. I've been shooting craps since I was a Girl Scout. I can't believe they didn't give merit badges for that.

VERA. Sad, but don't worry. We won't crash if I'm on board. I know the Lord's not through with me yet.

PEARL. Oh, I can't imagine why he wouldn't be.

VOICE OF THE PILOT. Folks, this is Captain Marlin Hooper. Hope you're enjoying your flight so far. We've only got five more stops to Vegas, and we're pretty sure we'll make it, but we do have a request that if there is a doctor on board, would you please ring your flight attendant call button, as we are in need of some medical assistance in the back of the plane. Thank you.

PEARL. Oh, I'm a midwife. I bet that pregnant woman in the back needs my help.

VERA. Don't get involved. You could get sued.

PEARL. But that woman might need help.

VERA. Oh, you know poor people; they have babies everywhere from Dennys to the line at Schlitterbahn. It's the only thing they're good at.

PEARL. How can you talk like that when you brought that square-headed hellion you call a son into this world?

VERA. Oh, did you get a bad batch of Geritol? You're babbling again.

PEARL. Vera, you're meaner than Mary Todd Lincoln.

VERA. You go so far back. What was she like?

(Hum of the engines indicates a passage of time. **VERA** *is looking out the window.)*

Mm. Mm-mm. Mm-mm-mm. Mm-mm-mm-mm-mm.

PEARL. Vera, you sound like you are passing a gallstone. What are you gruntin' about?

VERA. Flying over El Paso makes everything perfectly clear. Look, on our side of the border we've got freeways, traffic jams, Chucky Cheese, and a military base just brimmin' with weaponry: everything I love about America. And, just across the river, there's Mexico, just sitting there. They are entirely too close to us. Someone needs to ask them to move. Oh, that reminds me. I need to call my maid. She's watching my house for me while I'm out of town.

(**VERA** *pulls out a cell phone.*)

PEARL. Oh, my God, Vera! You can't use that. It will mess up the navigation system.

VERA. Oh, they just say that to kill time.

PEARL. Don't dial that phone. We could all end up on Fox News.

VERA. Oh, you're such an old worrywart.

(**VERA** *dials and the lights blow. Blackout. Out of the darkness comes the voice of the* **PILOT.**)

VOICE OF THE PILOT. Ladies and Gentlemen: this is captain Hooper again. If there is an electrician on the plane, would you please ring your flight attendant call button?

(*Lights up on* **PEARL** *and* **VERA.** *Both have oxygen masks on. The plane is making sputtering sounds.*)

PEARL. (*screams*) We're all going to die!!! (*pushes her flight attendant call button.*)

VERA. Oh, I better call my lawyer.

(**VERA** *dials. She removes her mask to talk, replacing it to take deep breaths.*)

PEARL. She's at it again!!

VERA. (*on her cellphone*) Wylie C.? Vera. I'm in a bit of a situation, and I want you to check my will to make sure that all my clothes, jewelry, and fragrances go to my sister,

VERA. *(cont.)* Phyllis. Make special note of foundation garments. I don't want to look down from heaven and catch Virgil prancing around in my high-end lingerie. I'm off: gotta pray now.

(She turns off the cell phone, and the sputtering sounds stop. **VERA** *and* **PEARL** *remove their masks.)*

Why, it stopped making that noise. I bet using that cell phone fixed whatever was wrong. Well, thank God for me. Oh, my God. I forgot to mention my hair curlers in my will.

(She digs out her cell phone.)

PEARL. No!!!

*(***VERA*** *dials, and the lights blow again. Blackout. Out of the darkness is heard the sound of the plane descending at high speed.)*

VOICE OF CARLOTTA. Ladies and Gentlemen: this is Captain Hooper again. If there is a drug dealer on the plane, would you please ring your flight attendant call button?

*(***VERA*** *and* **PEARL** *ride the sound of the descending plane in flickering lights. Tires screech. The Las Vegas sign flies in bouncing a couple of times before settling. Music: airport ambience.* **PEARL** *and* **VERA** *exit the plane and re-enter, minus their shoes, into the lobby of the Las Vegas Airport.)*

VERA. I can't believe they wouldn't let us wear our shoes on that emergency slide.

PEARL. Oh, and that flight attendant with the angel of death in her eyes saying: "Slide. It's fun."

VERA. I'll show them fun. Standing barefoot on these carpets that God knows who had walked on; I'll need my feet exfoliated.

PEARL. *(reaching into her bra for a coin)* Well, while we're waiting for them to bring our shoes, I'm going to try my luck.

*(***PEARL*** *drops a quarter in the slot machine and pulls the handle.)*

VERA. Oh, no you're not. We haven't been spared an untimely death just to have you mock Biblical law just the first chance you get, by gambling.

PEARL. I never read anything in the Bible about gambling.

(*PEARL drops a quarter in the slot machine and pulls the handle.*)

VERA. Oh, there's a coleslaw recipe in there, if you know where to look for it, and I'm not going to let you throw your money away like that.

(*PEARL drops a quarter in the slot machine and starts to pull the handle, but* **VERA** *grabs her hand and they struggle.*)

VERA. Don't do it. God's with me on this one.

PEARL. Don't make me bite you. I got off that plane alive. I know when I'm on a lucky streak.

VERA. I'll stop you if I end up in traction.

(*They both end up pulling the lever and the numbers whirl.*)

VERA. Well, don't blame me now that you're twenty-five cents poorer.

(*The machine hits Jackpot with lights, bells, whistles, and sirens, as massive amounts of coins spill out.* **VERA** *sinks to her knees to the floor.*)

It's a miracle! I won! I won!

(**VERA** *grovels on the floor for the money.*)

PEARL. Get back! Get back!

VERA. Oh, ye of little faith.

PEARL. I said: Get back!

VERA. Oh, happy, happy day!

PEARL. Get back! That's my money!

(**VERA** *growls.* **PEARL** *raises her cane to strike. Blackout*)

End of Act I

ACT II

Scene II, 1:
The Parking Lot of the Hula Chateaux Hotel,
Las Vegas, Nevada
Two days Later – Valentine's Day – Early that Morning

(HELEN and INITA are sitting in the front seat of their car, HELEN in the driver's seat. Just out of view is a flashing neon light, that floods the stage that goes on and off throughout the beginning of the scene until sunrise.)

INITA. I need to pee.

HELEN. Me too.

INITA. Why can't we get out of this car?

HELEN. Rattle snakes for one thing. And Joe Bob doesn't want a Security Guard to see us. He has to get a room and sneak us in, but we made it. Didn't we?

INITA. Yeah. *(She winces at the light flashing in her face.)* Is that what they mean when they go on about the lights of Las Vegas?

HELEN. I guess?

INITA. Damn. I can find that in Odessa. *(honks horn)* I need to pee.

HELEN. You're making it worse.

INITA. I can't believe we're sitting here in this lemon. The only thing that works on this car are the windshield wipers, and it hasn't rained a drop since we left Tuna.

HELEN. Oh cheer up, girl. So what if we had to buy five new tires and half a dozen hoses, and we lost first and second gears, and our clothes got stolen in Clovis, and I haven't slept in two days, and that snake got Joe Bob so hysterical people wouldn't stop and help, and we don't have any money or a way to get home, which is probably just as good, since I'm sure Vernon has fired us by now.

INITA. And we're out of Doritos.

HELEN. That was real selfish of Joe Bob to eat the last bag while he was pretending to be asleep. Still, we broke down right here in front of the Hula Chateaux Resort in lovely south downtown Las Vegas, didn't we? That's got to be lucky. I know it seems like we drove all the way to the end of the rainbow, and all we found was an empty pot,

INITA. If I had an empty pot I'd pee in it.

HELEN. Girl, you'd have to fight me for it. But we don't have one, and we can't let that depress us.

INITA. Well, what does it take to depress you, Helen? Shall we throw in a serial killer? For one thing, girl, you have to have rain to have a rainbow, and how you could even mention one, after we've been trapped in this car with Rosanne on diet pills in the back seat, singing Streisand and Judy Garland, is beyond me. I swear, if I ever lay eyes on a happy, little blue bird, I'll go at it with a pellet gun.

HELEN. Oh, I know. Or, people who need people.

*(Pause. **HELEN** opens her mouth to sing. All she gets out is "Peop…." **INITA** cuts her off.)*

INITA. Don't do it.

HELEN. I'm sorry. I guess I can't get it off my mind.

INITA. "People who need people." If he sings it one more time, he'll need people to load him into an ambulance. And Streisand can kiss me where the sun is not coming up tomorrow.

(The sun comes up and the lights from the blinking sign fade.)

HELEN. *(singing)* "Bet your bottom dollar…" Oh, look, the sun is coming up, just like you said it wouldn't. It's a sign.

INITA. Just don't sing about it. Please. *(She looks out the window.)* Do you see any rattle snakes?

HELEN. Not yet, but I'd let it get a bit lighter. *(sings)* "Oh, what a beautiful morning." See, there's something to be grateful for already. It's just like when we were waiting for that tow truck.

INITA. Which one?

HELEN. The one outside of Winslow.

INITA. Which one?

HELEN. The second one. Remember, we'd been in that gully for hours, and the first tow truck driver left us when Joe Bob freaked out about that snake, and I was trying to pump up that tire, and it was about 112 degrees, and Joe Bob started singing "People," and you went after him with that lug wrench, and he switched to, "With a Little Bit of Luck," and right then, when all seemed lost, right across the horizon came that tow truck with those two cute cowboys?

INITA. I liked that driver. He had pretty green eyes and looked like Johnny Chapel in the face.

HELEN. Without the scar.

INITA. Before that ax hit him.

HELEN. And those boys were real friendly.

INITA. Yeah, till Joe Bob brought up that weird cowboy movie and spooked 'em.

HELEN. They sure did get quiet, but the one Joe Bob and I rode into town with lightened up. By the time we hit Winslow, all three of us were singing, "I Enjoy Being a Girl."

INITA. Thank you God for leaving me with the quiet one.

HELEN. But, you see, Inita? The point is we are people who need people, even though we probably can't ever sing about it again, the sun will come up tomorrow and before the parade passes by, we'll just whistle a happy tune, and everything will come up roses.

INITA. Helen, you need to get some sleep. Wait. Do you smell that?

HELEN. I know. It's me. I need a shower.

INITA. No, it's bacon. Bacon! They're bound to have a breakfast buffet, and I'm going to crash it.

HELEN. No, Inita. Joe Bob said to wait here.

INITA. Yeah, while he eats up all the patty sausage and leaves the greasy links for us. I'm going. Joe Bob can stuff himself.

 (**INITA** *gets out of the car.*)

HELEN. Boy, you got that right.

 (**HELEN** *gets out of the car.*)

INITA. I really got to pee.

 (**INITA** *exits, changes to* **JOE BOB**.)

HELEN. Um-hmmmm....

 (**HELEN** *exits, changes to* **ANNA CONDA**.)

Scene II, 2:
Inside the Hula Chateau – Later that Morning

(Elevator doors close over an upstage center portal as lights come up to reveal the reception area of the Hula Chateau Hotel. A phone rings at the reception desk and is answered by a machine.)

VOICE ON MACHINE. *(voice of* **SHOT***)* You have reached the reservations desk of the Hula Chateau Resort and Spa in heart of scenic Downtown Las Vegas, where you are invited to relax in our semi-tropical Ug Wug Lounge, and for all you old timers who remember us back in the 50's as the Atomic Lodge, why not make yourself at home in our recently renovated Bombs Away Bar and Grill, where you can harken back to a simpler era when the Russians were the enemy and you could still smoke in elevators. And when night falls, you might want to have front row seats for our thrill a minute Undertow Cabaret, where ex-Broadway director Chuckey Whitebread nightly flaunts his disregard for all the rules of show business by working with children, live animals, fire-swallowing belly dancers. You have to see it to believe it.

(During above, **ANNA CONDA** *enters to behind reception desk and answers phone.)*

ANNA. Hula Chateau, Anna speaking. Why Mr. Gussow, how nice of you to call. How's the rash? Oh, what a shame. Yes, I'm in hot pursuit for our new floorshow director.

(Elevator bell dings and doors open, revealing **JOE BOB***, who enters.)*

No, Chucky had to go…When the belly dancer torched the peacock, I knew we'd crossed the Rubicon so to speak…I used to date a peacock rancher in Costa Rica. God, those birds have loud sex, sounds like Joan Rivers with the windows open.…Sorry, I forgot that was a sore spot. Oh yes, back to the floorshow

ANNA. *(cont.)* director, I'm looking for someone who can pursue diamond-bright concepts on a crape paper budget. Some shtick-pedaling fool, who's crazy enough to try anything.... And I think I've got someone in mind. Oh, don't worry. We'll have a show up tomorrow.... Bye, now. You remember to keep those sore spots exposed to fresh air. Tah-tah. *(She hangs up.)* Little worm. *(She looks at* **JOE BOB**.*)* You are hired.

JOE BOB. What?

ANNA. Allow me to introduce myself, my name is Anna Conda.

JOE BOB. I'm Joe Bob Lipsey.

ANNA. I know all about you, dear. You just arrived from.... I'm a Gemini. Help me here.

JOE BOB. Texas?

ANNA. I was going to say New Mexico.

JOE BOB. I was in the Red Dirt Theater Festival in Ruidoso.

ANNA. Of course, you were, dear. I performed there myself years ago. I think I'm safe in saying I was the funniest Hedda Gabler this side of Australia.

JOE BOB. Just hearing you talk about it gives me goose bumps.

ANNA. Of course it does, dear. *(snort)* You've come out here to start a new life after the thorns that have pricked you artistically.

JOE BOB. Boy, have I been pricked.

ANNA. I can see that. You're grand.

JOE BOB. Yes.

ANNA. You deserve better.

JOE BOB. Yes.

ANNA. And all you ever needed was the budget to prove how brilliant you really are.

JOE BOB. Yes.

ANNA. It's always been your dream to see it done here in Las Vegas: The New Broadway, the Broadway without an intermission, where you will rule.

JOE BOB. Yes.

ANNA. Because you're so brilliant.

JOE BOB. I am.

ANNA. And talented.

JOE BOB. That's me.

ANNA. And broke.

JOE BOB. How did you know?

ANNA. I saw you stuffing bacon in your briefs. You don't do that if you're carrying a Gold Card. So what do you have in mind for your premier production? Something outrageous? Something mindless and duh-duh?

JOE BOB. Yes.

ANNA. All you need is a cast and some showgirls to boss around.

JOE BOB. Yes, and I travel with two showgirls who need work and can be bossed around.

ANNA. It's a shame they're not female impersonators. You can get them to work for lip-gloss as long as the lighting's right.

JOE BOB. These two will pass for impersonators.

ANNA. *(snort)* You are a genius. Female impersonators who are real females: that's the kind of thinking that this country hungers for. I could kiss your hem.

JOE BOB. Be my guest.

ANNA. Well it's a figure of speech, dear. This is a tourist town. Germs, germs. I'll call Shot and tell him we've found our new floorshow director.

JOE BOB. I'll run out to the car and get my show tune collection.

ANNA. You do that, dear. Chop, chop.

> **(JOE BOB** *exits by way of the elevator and changes to* **LEONARD. ANNA** *dials the phone.)*
>
> Shot, darling, I found our new floorshow director.... Oh, just like all the others. He walked in off the street.... To quote Bugs Bunny: "What a maroon!" .... Oh yes, dear, we'll save a bundle. This one is the type

ANNA. *(cont.)* who will work for carbohydrates…. Love you, too…. Yes, we'll always have Spokane. Tah-tah, my little furry Valentine.

(**ANNA** *hangs up. The phone rings; after breath,* **ANNA** *answers it.*)

Front desk. Anna speaking.

(**LEONARD** *enters, calling from his room.*)

LEONARD. This is Leonard Childers. I've got to find a bail bondsman. My wife has been arrested.

ANNA. Fortunately, we have a number on call. I must ask. Did your wife's problem spring from violence, moral turpitude, or traffic?

LEONARD. She was stuffing dollar bills down some male wee-wee dancer's underwear. She slipped in a twenty by mistake and went back for change.

ANNA. Oops.

LEONARD. Now, he claims she grabbed more than the money, and he's probably got a case, because Reba can be damn mean, when she thinks she's been gypped.

ANNA. And where were you during all this grunting and growling?

LEONARD. I was flat on my back with my hiatal hernia.

ANNA. Oh, that's my least favorite kind. *(snort)* Now I'm going to put you through to Back-in-a-Flash Bail Bonds. Ask for Smokey Trulock, he's a local legend with russet-sized cajones. In the old days he'd climb out of bed at all hours to spring anyone who took a swing at Sinatra. Some day they'll name a street after him.

LEONARD. I appreciate it.

ANNA. Of course you do, dear. And tell Smokey, Anna says, "We'll always have Walla Walla.

(*Both hang up.* **LEONARD** *exits.* **ANNA** *looks at the Guest Registry.*)

Well, I need to do a sucker check of the Registry. Pearl Burras, she's that old relic in the Titan Suite who won the jackpot. It may be hard to shake any change out of that one. That's a triple Taurus, if I ever saw one. *(She sees something in the Register that bothers her.)* Oh no! Petey Fisk, Tuna Texas Humane Society. *(snort)* I smell a rat. Better call Ricky. *(She dials.)* Ricky, what's the condition of that peacock's burns? Well, we have someone registered from the Humane Society. Could be a spy. If he stumbles across that burnt bird, it will be like the ides of March without the togas. I can't go through that again.

(SHOT enters.)

ANNA. *(cont.)* Well, comprende, you're dead meat on a hook if you fail in your responsibility to slap Noxzema on that bird's burnt ass every hour on the hour. *(She glances at her watch.)* Oh, my, Ricky. It's eight-fifty nine. Tick, tick, tick, tick. *(She hangs up. To phone.)* Wimp. *(to SHOT)* Shot, will you be the lamb chop that you are and watch the desk? I need to burn a Newport; then I'm going to center my spirit and float with my inner angel before I come back and chew a hole in Ricky's useless ass.

SHOT. I'd like to watch that.

(ANNA pushes elevator call button, enters elevator when doors open.)

ANNA. Well, of course you can. I know what that does to you.

(ANNA growls at him seductively, doors close and she exits and changes to VERA. SHOT calls after her.)

SHOT. You make me weak in the ankles. Weak in the ankles. You know that? When a woman like that knows how to push your buttons, you're like putty in her hands, putty, putty. She can work me like Play dough. *(He calls on his cell phone.)* Hey Rickey, you have any more trouble from that mean woman with the pussycat glasses? Yeah, she's steamed 'cause we had to toss her from the Titan Suite and move her to the Edgar Allen Poe down in the basement. Keep your wallet in your front

SHOT. *(cont.)* pocket around that one. I know a habitual when I see one. She wants a refund? Yeah right. Let her call me if she's got the ovaries. *(He hangs up.)*

(The reception desk phone rings. **SHOT** *answers it.)*

Front Desk. You got Shot.

(Enter **VERA CARP** *on phone.)*

VERA. I'm calling to complain about the pendulum in the Edgar Allen Poe suite.

SHOT. What's wrong with it?

VERA. It doesn't swing. That's what's wrong with it.

SHOT. It's not supposed to. It's decorative.

VERA. Well maybe where you come from pendulums just hang there, but in Texas we expect them to swing, and I demand a refund. Hang on; I've got a woman working on my feet. *(speaking to the woman)* Senorita, no lo touchie el corn. Corn... Corn. Massa. *(to* **SHOT***)* There she goes, we've been through this all day; she'll be back in ten minutes with a plate of hot tortillas. Okay, back to my refund, cash will do nicely.

SHOT. Cash? Lady, you're trying to shake me down for gambling money.

VERA. What a vicious thing to say about me. I may have to sue you unless we can reach a settlement. Make an offer.

SHOT. Lady, you don't scare me. I've got friends who are mobsters.

VERA. Oh please, I can beat that. I've got friends who are Southern Baptists.

SHOT. I'll slip a fifty under your door.

VERA. Don't keep me waiting.

(Both hang up. **SHOT** *exits and changes to* **BERTHA***.* **VERA** *dials.)*

VERA. This is Vera Carp. Get my husband on the line. W.H., did you sell the china? Wonderful, send me the money quick. I've got a hot tip on a thoroughbred. We can double that and have a kitty left for roulette. Oh W.H., stop whining. Your great, great grandmother's been dead forever. Why would she care if we got rid of all those tacky old dishes from Dresden? Now did you sell the silver? No takers? Well, put a sign around your neck and stand on the bridge at Juarez like I told you to. What kind of a businessman are you? You don't want to sell it? Why? For sentimental reasons? W.H., you'll be sentimental for your thumb when that guy named Guido shows up and takes one, 'cause that's what's going to happen if you don't get him the scratch by Friday. Have you ever tried to hold a fork with four fingers? You are so emotional. Hey, you signed up for better or worse, so be a man. Look, I've got to go collect my refund. Why don't you call me back, W.H., after you've grown a pair?

(VERA hangs up and exits and changes to PETEY. Lights cross fade to Titan Suite as elevator doors open. Pearl's phone in the Titan suite rings. PEARL enters and answers it)

PEARL. Hello. Oh, Henry. Thank God, you're back!... Well, you've got to get out to Vegas, quick, quick, quick... I'm in a crisis. Don't you yell at me or I'll never clip your toenails again. *(pause)* No. I didn't forget my luger.... No. Nobody has molested me, but I appreciate the thought. I won a huge jackpot. We're rich. Isn't that awful? The IRS will be on us like vultures. And, it gets worse.... What's worse than the IRS? Every time I fall asleep I dream I've turned into Vera Carp. You need to get out here and help me get rid of this money. We need the write offs. I know you haven't been on a plane since you bombed the Red Chinese, but this is an emergency. *(She hangs up. There is a knock at the door.)* Go away!

(Enter PETEY.)

PETEY. Hi, Mrs. Burras. Could I have a moment of your time?

PEARL. Petey. Don't you understand human? I said, go away?

PETEY. I'll just be a minute. I'm here to appeal to your generosity and solicit a contribution toward my efforts to rescue an exploited peacock.

(**PEARL** *gasps and waves away misfortune.*)

PEARL. Peacock! Oh, they're the worst bad luck in the entire animal kingdom.

PETEY. That's an old wives' tale.

PEARL. You be nice to old wives. They get a bad rap.

PETEY. Only their tail feathers are considered bad luck, and Reggie's all got burned off in a lounge act gone bad.

PEARL. Oh, the poor unlucky bird. All my laying hens got their feathers blown off, when a twister touched down right next to their coop.

PETEY. Did they grow back?

PEARL. Yes. But the psychological damage was done. Some of them still won't cluck. I know a good cause when I see it. Petey, get that bird on a private jet to Texas, and have them bill my room.

PETEY. As one bird lover to another, may I say your generosity is only exceeded by your innate sense of kindness.

PEARL. Go away!

PETEY. Right.

(**PETEY** *exits and changes to* **MAURICE.** *The phone rings.* **PEARL** *answers.*)

PEARL. Hello. Anna? You've got me pulling out my hair. Stop calling. No. I don't need a beautician. I need you to stop sending people up here. *(She hangs up.)* If one more person knocks, I'll have a rigger. *(There's a knock at the door. She has a rigger. She yells.)* Go away!

(**MAURICE** *enters.*)

MAURICE. Mrs. Burr-ass, Maurice.

PEARL. That's Burras, Morris.

MAURICE. It's Maurice. Elongate the second syllable.

PEARL. Mau…rice.

MAURICE. That's a little better. I'm here to do something about your hair.

PEARL. I don't have any hair. I told Anna that.

MAURICE. Yes. You have that classic Missouri look. If you were a movie, Judy Dench would play you. Now, let me have a peak under there. *(He lifts the hat slightly from behind to peak and screams.)* Ahhhhhh! Lord, girl, there's nothing there. It's like Brokeback Mountain without the sheep. Now, you need to listen to an expert. We need to glue that hat down, and then we're going to load you down with lots of jewelry, low-hanging necklaces, anything to keep people from looking up. I'll see what we have in stock, and we'll bill you.

PEARL. Bill me? I may be rich, but I'm not handing over money to a hairdresser. I told you. I don't have any hair.

MAURICE. Don't get Leona Helmsly with me. God, you old rich girls are all alike. The consultation is free.

(MAURICE exits and changes to WO-HU.)

PEARL. Well, I guess I won't be sending any money to the Benevolent Hairburner's Fund.

(Phone rings. PEARL answers.)

PEARL. Hello? Anna, you've got to get these people out of here. I'm coming apart at the seams…. No. I don't need a tailor…. Of course, I sound tense!… I'm so worked up; I'm ready to walk down the street and hurl myself off the Eiffel Tower…. You're going to send up a what?… An acupuncturist?…Why?… To calm me down?… I can assure you: nothing will calm me down less than a Chinese woman sticking needles in me. Go away! *(She hangs up. Knock)* Go away!

(Enter WO-HU [pronounced "woe-who"].)

WO-HU. Hello. Time for acupuncture. My name is Wo-Hu, but you just call me Hu.

PEARL. Who?

WO-HU. Yes.

PEARL. Yes, what?

WO-HU. Not what. Hu.

PEARL. Who?

WO-HU. Me.

PEARL. You?

WO-HU. I Hu.

PEARL. You who?

WO-HU. *(She waves at her.)* And yoo-hoo, too.

PEARL. That's an unusual first name. What's your last name?

WO-HU. Schnikleheimer. My husband's from Switzerland. When he get a little horny, he go: "Oh, da-lay-he-hoo." He makes me laugh. Ha, ha, ha, ha. But, back to acupuncture. *(circling Pearl to survey her)* Oh, you a full-figure girl. Gonna take a lotta needle. I be back in a hurry. Please, take off all your clothes.

PEARL. Who do you think you are?

WO-HU. Hu. How many times do I have to tell you?

PEARL. *(loudly)* Go away!!

WO-HU. Bye, bye.

*(**WO-HU** exits and changes to **ANNA**.)*

PEARL. Oh, I need to calm down. Maybe I'll watch television.

*(**PEARL** clicks on remote and we hear sleazy music.)*

VOICES ON TV. "Fred, Fred." "Oh, you betcha." "Oh, what are you gonna do with that?" "Put on the hat, baby! Can you chuckle like a squirrel?" "Anything, for you, Fred." "Don't tip over. Gotcha!" "Ohhhhhhh."

PEARL. *(over above)* Oh, that's disgusting. She should put some iodine on that. *(as she sits)* I ought to turn that off. *(There's a knock at the door.)* Go away!

*(Enter **ANNA**.)*

ANNA. It's me, dear.

*(**PEARL** turns off the TV.)*

I can see you're much too busy to bother with the door. I can send Ricky up to do that for you.

PEARL. God, no. Anna, how can you afford to treat people this nice?

ANNA. Oh, you must never equate yourself with something as pedestrian as people. You're loaded now, so act like it. To do otherwise would invite bad luck.

PEARL. You'll bring down a curse talking like that. Quick. Spin in a circle three times.

ANNA. By all means.

(She spins in a circle three times.)

PEARL. I don't want to be rich. I don't know how to act like it.

ANNA. Oh, it's simple, dear. Leave the price tags on long enough to intimidate the second cousins, then start with the finger food. I'll have some Russian caviar sent up. That reminds me of the time I dined with Nina Krushchev in Mermansk. Oh, she was a big girl. She ate whale blubber with her fingers and never got my punch lines, but the old gal was a hell-of-a musician.

PEARL. Really.

ANNA. Oh, you get enough potato vodka in her, she'd grab her balalaika and zip out the minute waltz in fifty-two seconds. Most impressive. *(snort)* Now, I assume you want to upgrade your nieces wedding to something slightly more upscale. She bought our basic package. We call it the compassionate conservative. It means absolutely nothing, but it feels so good to say it.

PEARL. I want to hire an Elvis impersonator for the wedding.

ANNA. Splendid. I know just the agency.

PEARL. Tell them I want the top of the line. I saw an Elvis on the street that looked like Newt Gingrich.

ANNA. Frightening.

PEARL. And he has to sing "Love Me Tender." It's Valentine's.

ANNA. I got married once to "Jailhouse Rock," but to each his own, and I can cut you a deal on our professional stand in bridesmaid. You saw her last night; the sultry girl with the tattoos. *(snort)*

PEARL. Damn. She looked mean.

ANNA. No. Just bitter. Comes with the job. You know: always a bridesmaid. And due to child labor laws, we can't provide you with a flower girl, but we have a lovely little dwarf on call.

PEARL. How old is she?

ANNA. Well, she passes for thirty in candlelight. Well, I better go book that dwarf. It'd be a shame to lose her.

PEARL. You're too good to me, Anna.

ANNA. Of course I am, dear. *(snort)*

(**ANNA** *exits and changes to* **DIDI**. **PEARL** *picks up a remote control device.*)

PEARL. Oh, I haven't seen this before.

(She pushes a button. The lights fade and soft, love-making music comes on at a low level. She looks around to see if anyone is watching.)

Oh, that'll come in handy, when Henry gets here..

(There's a knock at the door. She pushes a button which restores the lights and turns off the music.)

Go away!

(Enter **DIDI**.*)*

DIDI. Well, well, well. Put on some lipstick and kiss my ass. All this fancy rigmarole, because you pulled the right lever at the right time, in the right place, right in the middle of Las-freakin'-Vegas, all I can say is kiss my ass!

PEARL. Oh, it's a fate worst than death. How could this happen to a nice old lady like me?

DIDI. You must still be in shock, Pearl. You're sounding goofy as mamma. She still thinks she won the Pick-A-Pet Bingo pot.

PEARL. You'll have to bring her up here to eat my buffet.

DIDI. Oh, no. Mamma's pretty much down to soup and Jello. Truman was in the White House, when she lost her last tooth.

PEARL. Oh, I'm sure I could mash something up for her.

DIDI. No, no. It's best not to feed her. She'll come down quicker.

PEARL. Oh, Didi, that money's a curse. The IRS already knows about it. They'll be on me like freckles.

DIDI. God….damn them! Just because the country needs roads and bridges and an army and a navy and an air force and thousands of nuclear weapons and more prisons and a border fence and enough juice to warm up the electric chair, they want to pay for it out of my pocket. God…damn. Explain to me how that's fair.

PEARL. And it gets worse.

DIDI. Worse than the IRS? Pearl, you're going Daffy Duck on me.

PEARL. I dreamed I turned into Vera Carp.

DIDI. God….damn! That is worse than the IRS. Speaking of her, you're going to need a bodyguard.

PEARL. Oh, I'll be fine.

DIDI. I don't know, Vera's claiming half that pot. She's in her element here. She can get you killed for a pack of Camels.

PEARL. Oh, my God. It's half past the hour… Time for me to take my good luck shower.

DIDI. You need to shake off those superstitions, Pearl.

PEARL. Oh, if I miss my shower it might start raining Chinese babies.

(**PEARL** *exits and changes to* **SHOT**.)

DIDI. Well, we don't want that.

PEARL. *(off stage)* Keep an eye on the door, Didi.

DIDI. Don't you worry about squat, Pearl.

(**DIDI** *picks up the same remote and the lights fade and music comes on.* **DIDI** *looks about puzzled and pushes another button and the lights are restored and the music stops. She pushes the remote again and the lights repeat their pattern complete with soft music. She hums along, interrupted by a long drag on her cigarette. There is a knock at the door.* **DIDI** *pushes the remote again and the lights restore and the music ends.)*

DIDI. *(cont.)* Come in.

    (**SHOT** *enters.*)

    Freeze! Up against the wall! Spread em! *(She frisks him.)* Are you looking for Pearl?

SHOT. Yeah, who are you?

DIDI. I'm asking the questions. Who are you?

SHOT. Name's Shot. Whom are you?

DIDI. I'm her bodyguard. Shot, I'll need your identification.

SHOT. This is a private floor. I'm afraid I'm going to have to see some identification from you.

DIDI. Don't let your mouth write a check your body can't cash. I'm a real Tie Won Toe yellow belt. My husband drove me to it, he ran off with aliens.

SHOT. Oh, yeah? I had a wife who did that.

DIDI. R.R. left on a spaceship headed for the moon.

SHOT. She left in a Chevy heading for Mexico.

DIDI. I'll never get over it.

SHOT. Yeah. Well I'm holding up. Here's my I.D. I'm what you call your incognito hotel security guard.

DIDI. I could get into that line of work, but I'd wind up killing someone. Damn near killed my husband once, mistook him for a quail. Sad. I never got another shot.

SHOT. Yeah. I almost killed my wife once. It's not easy.

DIDI. No, it's not. So you work for the hotel, huh?

SHOT. Yeah, I've been here all my life. I'm a desert man really. I need a little sand in my face.

DIDI. I can see that. Well, Pearl's in the shower, you'll have to come back later.

SHOT. It was good talking to ya, there… Miss…?

DIDI. Snavely. Didi Snavely.

SHOT. Don't worry about Mrs. Burras. Yeah, we keep a good eye on the big winners here. Between you and me she's safe as a kitten.

DIDI. Say, this is some fancy hotel, ain't it? Old Blue Eyes is the only thing missing.

SHOT. He's the one who shot me!

DIDI. Sinatra shot you?

SHOT. Yeah, that's how I got the name Shot. He shot me in the butt. I don't remember it; I was just a baby.

DIDI. Sinatra shot you in the butt?

SHOT. Yeah, he was cleaning his gun, and my old man had brought me to work that day, and it was all a mix-up, but I became somebody. I was the baby shot by Frank Sinatra; it used to be a big deal around here.

DIDI. Well I'll be. Can I get your autograph?

SHOT. Oh no. You're gonna embarrass me.

DIDI. You know, I spent seven hours at that gun show today, and I could tell that every man that hit on me was a clear cut case of all trigger and no barrel, and right here in the hotel is a guy who got shot by Sinatra.

SHOT. You shouldn't go to the gun show on Valentine's Day, without a male escort, a nice woman like you.

DIDI. Well, nobody's asked me.

SHOT. What am I? Chopped liver?

DIDI. That's the most romantic thing anybody's ever said to me.

SHOT. Let's take in the gun show, and then I'll show you where I got shot.

DIDI. That's a bit much on the first date, isn't it? I'm a Baptist.

SHOT. No, no. I meant the hotel. It's still there.

(They both laugh.)

I'm off at seven. I'll give you a call.

DIDI. You do that, Shot. You do that, and I'll be waiting.

*(***SHOT*** exits and changes to **ELVIS 11**. **DIDI** lights a cigarette and starts singing the romantic song that had been playing. She takes a drag, continuing the lyrics in her head, and ends singing the last few words.* **DIDI** exits and changes to **ELVIS 42**.)*

---

*See Music Use Note on Page 3.

Scene II, 3:
The Hotel Lobby – Later that Afternoon

*(The elevator doors close after **DIDI**'s exit. The bell rings and the elevator doors open and **ELVIS 11**, an impersonator from the sequined white stretch-pants era, enters. The elevator doors close, the bell rings again and the doors reopen and **ELVIS 42**, another impersonator, "Blue Hawaii" period, enters. He spots **ELVIS 11**.)*

ELVIS 11. What are you doing here?

ELVIS 42. What are you doing here?

ELVIS 11. I asked you first.

ELVIS 42. I asked you second.

ELVIS 11. Did Marsha send you?

ELVIS 42. Maybe. Who sent you?

ELVIS 11. None of your beeswax. Well, I just hope you're not thinking you got the 7:30 wedding, 'cause if she double-booked I've got seniority.

ELVIS 42. Says who?

ELVIS 11. Says me.

ELVIS 42. It don't matter what you say.

ELVIS 11. Does too.

ELVIS 42. Does not.

ELVIS 11. Does too.

ELVIS 42. Does not

ELVIS 11. Uh-huh.

ELVIS 42. Nuh-uh.

ELVIS 11. Uh-huh.

ELVIS 42. Nuh-uh.

ELVIS 11.	**ELVIS 42.**
Uh-huh.	Nuh-uh.
Uh-huh.	Nuh-uh.
Uh-huh.	Nuh-uh.
Uh-huh.	Nuh-uh.
Uh-huh.	Nuh-uh.

(Speaking faster and faster until **ELVIS 11** *starts coughing.)*

ELVIS 42. You seem a little winded there, Pard. I hope you're not planning to sing anything tougher than "In the Ghetto."

ELVIS 11. You Blue Hawaii assholes are all alike. Well, a few more years of deep-fat-fried fig-newton-cream-cheese Monte Christos and we'll see how you look in them passion flower swim trunks.

ELVIS 42. *(with a bit of a swagger)* Well, I don't really need this gig. I got more work than I can handle. It's just the principle of the thing.

ELVIS 11. Well, if it's just the principle, why don't you just scoot off and have some "fun in Acapulco" and let a poor old man make his Cadillac payment?

ELVIS 42. Is that your titty-pink caddy out there? Oh, mama: I'd kill to have that car.

ELVIS 11. Five hundred dollars and she's yours, and I'll throw in the jumper cables, 'cause you're sure as hell going to need them.

ELVIS 42. She gotta lot a miles on her?

ELVIS 11. I quit counting.

ELVIS 42. I drive me a Plymouth Duster. She's got so many miles, I call her Joan Collins.

ELVIS 11. Hell. That's funny.

ELVIS 42. Well, this thing with Marsha is getting totally out of hand.

ELVIS 11. Sure as hell is.

ELVIS 42. Last week I played a bunch of dental hygienists and she sent me an Ann Margaret that only had four teeth.

ELVIS 11. Damn. I hate it when that happens.

ELVIS 42. Ooh, she looked like a pocket comb from North Arkansas. All we got in the tip jar was dental floss.

ELVIS 11. I feel your pain, son. Last week she booked me for a Tupperware convention.

ELVIS 42. Oh God, how bad was it?

ELVIS 11. You know when those gals get hungry they'll turn on you. I went flat just a little bit on "Hunka Hunka Burnin' Love," and they pulled out their samples and burped me off the stage.

ELVIS 42. Oh, that's cold. Well, you know who's in town next week.

ELVIS 11. Who?

ELVIS 42. Morticians.

ELVIS 11. Oh hell, I'd rather die.

ELVIS 42. Be careful what you wish for. I'm calling Marsha. I smell a rat.

ELVIS 11. Uh-huh.

(**ELVIS 42** *dials his cell phone. He speaks in a real Elvis voice.*)

ELVIS 42. Marsha…It's me…It's me…Elvis…Number 42. Gal, you double-booked me again. *(to* **ELVIS 11***)* What's your number?

ELVIS 11. Eleven.

ELVIS 42. *(back to Elvis voice)* Eleven. Well, this has happened a whole lot lately, and I don't mind telling you, I'm all shook up about it.

ELVIS 11. Don't be cruel.

ELVIS 42. What? They cancelled? Well, can we split the deposit? Let me tell you something, little sister, that really scuffs up my blue suede shoes, and you ain't no friend of mine. *(He hangs up.)*

ELVIS 11. Son, if I were you, I'd count to twenty and call her back, or you're going to be playing bingo parlors in Parumph.

ELVIS 42. Right, Pard.

ELVIS 11. Well, I hope I got enough gas to get me to the next gig. *(He pushes elevator call button.)*

ELVIS 42. You working the psychiatrists?

ELVIS 11. Other end. Proctologists.

(The elevator doors open. **ELVIS** 11 *steps inside.)*

ELVIS 42. I hear they tip out the butt.

ELVIS 11. Let's hope so.

*(***ELVIS** 11 *poses. The elevator doors close, and he exits and changes to* **INITA.** **ELVIS** 42 *dials his cell phone.)*

ELVIS 42. *(In his Elvis voice)* Marsha, it's me again, number 42. No. No. It's all right, Mama. Now…now…now, who's your Teddy Bear? Sure, I'll do you a favor. Sure. Who you want me to play? *(pause)* Who? The morticians? And you'll send the same Ann Margaret? God… bless you. I've got something to ask you too. Say, are you lonesome tonight? How about I come over a little later and sing "Daddy's Home"?…Hello…Hello… Ever' time I'm getting somewhere with a woman this cell phone craps out.

*(***ELVIS** 42 *pushes the elevator call button, the doors open, he enters dialing cell phone.)*

Hello, Marsha, it's me. It's me.

(The doors close. **ELVIS** 42 *exits and changes to* **HELEN.** *The elevator music, an Elvis tune, swells and fades.)**

---

* *See Music Use Note on Page 3.

Scene II, 4:
The Undertow Cabaret – That Evening

(We hear **PERRY FELCHER** *from backstage. He punctuates his speech with drum rolls and rim shots.)*

VOICE OF PERRY. Welcome Forks and Spoons. This is Perry Felcher, the voice of the Undertow Cabaret, the venue that brought you the groundbreaking dancing of Snuffy Demint, South Carolina's only one-legged clogger. When Snuffy hits the stage, you don't know whether to laugh or cry. And now, please welcome our new artistic director, Joe Bob Lipsey, whose shows have stunned audiences from Waco to Flagstaff and two places in between, as he brings us his extravaganza with a question mark, "Is She, or Isn't She?"

(Soft, up-beat music plays. The elevator doors open, revealing a rain curtain. **HELEN** *and* **INITA** *enter through the rain curtain in showgirl costumes.* **INITA***'s costume represents winter on front with snowmen breasts with carrot noses and autumn on back with a life size turkey on her behind.* **HELEN***'s represents spring on front with flowers that spin and summer on back with fly swatters and such.)*

INITA. I hate this. I hate this. I hate this rehearsing.

HELEN. We have to get to work. We've gotta have that paycheck to get home on.

INITA. I can't do that dance step, Helen.

HELEN. Oh, it's easy, girl. Look. *(She does the step.)* Ta-dah!

INITA. I can do the ta-dah.

HELEN. Joe Bob will spit blood from his eyeballs if you just do the ta-dah.

INITA. I'll do the ta-dah on the top of his head with a high heel.

HELEN. Okay, okay, just do the ta-dah.

INITA. I'll do the ta-dah.

HELEN. Just do the ta-dah.

INITA. Ta-dah.

HELEN. Fine. Now, let's move on to the fabulous turning of the seasons.

(They strike poses.)

She looks fabulous in the spring time. *(She turns.)* She looks fabulous in the summer.

(She turns back and points at **INITA** *who turns.)*

She looks fabulous in the fall.

*(**INITA** stops performing.)*

What's wrong?

INITA. I can't stand it. These shoes are coming off.

HELEN. Kill the music, Perry, and give us a few minutes.

*(The music stops. **INITA** takes her shoes off.)*

PERRY'S VOICE. I'll be in the bar, if you need me.

HELEN. Perry, change the steak on Joe Bob's eye while you are in there. *(to **INITA**)* I can't believe you punched Joe Bob out. What did he say to set you off?

INITA. I'm not talking.

HELEN. Come on girl. It's me.

INITA. Dick Cheney couldn't get it out of me with a rubber hose, and girl, if it wasn't for your bright ideas, we'd be home now, but you had to drag us barefoot through hell to go to a gay rodeo.

HELEN. How was I to know?

INITA. It said gay rodeo on the poster.

HELEN. I didn't know it was that kind of gay. I thought it was la la la la happy gay.

INITA. It was la la la la happy gay. Men in wigs, barrel racing? When he got off that horse, his falsies were pointing backwards.

HELEN. Well, we'll be home soon and back at work.

INITA. If there's any business left. Vernon hired the Palvadore Sisters to work the restaurant while we were gone.

HELEN. *(Suddenly crestfallen)* Candy and Taffy?

INITA. Yeah. And Taffy stopped for a smoke break during lunch rush and sat on the grill. They had to close down the restaurant and take her to the clinic.

HELEN. And Candy's waiting tables? Girl, nobody's going to warm up to a waitress with an eye patch. (**HELEN** *starts to cry.*)

INITA. *(worried)* Helen?

HELEN. What's she going to say when she brings you your change? "Y'all come back; I'll keep an eye out for ya." I got us into this.

INITA. Helen?

HELEN. *(beginning to sob)* I'm a bad person.

INITA. Oh, God. It's starting.

HELEN. Momma always said I was as dumb as a waffle iron.

INITA. Please! Don't bring up your momma.

HELEN. She said I didn't have the brains to crack an egg.

INITA. Helen, cracking eggs is harder than it looks.

HELEN. I'm to blame for the fire at the beauty college.

INITA. Oh, God! Here we go. All you did was toss away a cigarette. How were you to know that's where they kept the spray net?

HELEN. And I'm the reason Carley Hickey went to prison.

INITA. What?

HELEN. I told him blue was his color and right after that is when he stole that baby blue thunderbird.

INITA. Stop it, Helen! Carley Hickey's baby picture was a mug shot. I've seen it. Look here, girl, what about that really cute cowboy that hit on you at the rodeo? That's something.

HELEN. No, it's not. He thought I was a drag queen. *(sobs)*

INITA. Stop it, Helen!

HELEN. No, I won't. You had that BIG ol' guy ask you out.

INITA. Helen, that wasn't a guy. Her name was Shelia.

HELEN. All the women at that rodeo were named Shelia. I've never been to a rodeo where the men wear perfume and women fistfight in the parking lot. It's supposed to be the other way around.

INITA. Helen, you've got to stop crying.

HELEN. I can't.

INITA. If you stop, I'll tell you why I punched out Joe Bob.

HELEN. *(suddenly bright-eyed)* Okay.

INITA. He told me that if I wanted to pass as a female impersonator, I'd have to do a better job at shaving my back, and I hit him right in the eye.

HELEN. And when he comes to, he's going to fire us. *(She starts crying again.)*

INITA. Helen, I'm going to get us out of this. *(She takes out her cell phone.)* Now, who do we know that has money?

(They look into space thinking, then at each other.)

HELEN & INITA. Aunt Pearl!

HELEN. Give me that cell phone. *(She grabs the phone from* **INITA** *and dials.)* Hi, Miss Burras. It's Helen…Oh, I'm not calling for any particular reason. I just wanted to chat…No, I just wanted to congratulate you on your jackpot and remind you I am not to blame for that bad can of beans…and see how you're feeling and ask if you can give me and Inita enough money to get back to Tuna…You'll put us on a private jet with Petey…Oh, no problem…No, we don't mind sitting by a peacock… Oh, thank you so much, Miss Burras. You'll never pay for another French fry for the rest of your life. Bye.

(She hangs up. To **INITA** *as she exits.)*

Girl, you are going to get on that plane, you're not going to scream, "We're all gonna die," and you're going to have to sit next to a peacock.

*(**HELEN** exits and changes to **ARLES**.)*

INITA. That's not a problem. I've been walking around all day with a turkey on my ass.

*(**INITA** exits and changes to **BERTHA**.)*

Scene II, 5:
Back Home in Tuna – That Night

(During below, elevator doors close, rain curtain is removed, and doors reopen as scene lights come up at **BERTHA** *and* **ARLES**' *home back in Tuna.)*

VOICE OF COLONEL SPRAYBERRY. This is Colonel Hollis Sprayberry with a question for all concerned parents: Are your kids so out of control they've got you hiding out under the sink? Do they have enough tattoos to pass for wallpaper and so many piercings they whistle when the wind picks up? Well, send that mouthy young'un off for a full week at Colonel Sprayberry's Survival Institute and Boot-in-the-Butt Character Camp. We'll teach your kids how to identify the warning signs of radical, political moderation and how to disrupt public discourse regardless of the facts at hand. How 'bout a crash course on intolerance in the scriptures? And my own personal favorite: "Making Friends through Waterboarding." So, sign up your kids for a week at Colonel Sprayberry's. Don't worry, when you get your kids back, they'll still be mean, but they'll be mean for all the right reasons.

(During above, **ARLES** *enters in a bad modo, fixes a drink, then turns off the radio.)*

ARLES. God, it's good to be home. Well, I'll tell you, it's a hell of a note when you have to leave your vacation early so you can get away from the people you know.

*(***BERTHA*** enters in a bad mood and continues unpacking a suitcase.)*

BERTHA. I know. Well, I'm almost unpacked, just one more bag. What is this?

ARLES. What?

BERTHA. This orange plastic thing.

ARLES. I told you I was going to spread out a tarp in the hotel room and squirt you with a water pistol if that's what it took to get you in that swimsuit. The squirt gun's in there somewhere. You were so upset about that vibrating bed; I thought I better just let it pass.

BERTHA. Don't bring it up. I never heard of such a thing, dropping a quarter into a slot and the bed starts shaking like a faith healer.

ARLES. It said on the thing that bed emitted a soothing calming vibration.

BERTHA. That's a lie. It knocked pictures off the wall. That's as close to an earthquake as I intend to get. I've still got a charley horse from hiding in that bathtub.

ARLES. I didn't scare you on purpose. I know how you are about that.

BERTHA. I'll get you back, and it'll be worse than last time.

ARLES. What could be worse than flipping off the lights while I'm taking a shower and putting on the music to "Psycho"? I've been taking tub baths for six months.

BERTHA. You knew better than to sneak up behind me and kiss me on the neck when I'm watching a vampire movie.

ARLES. I wasn't sneaking.

BERTHA. If I don't hear you, it's sneaking.

ARLES. Well, what am I supposed to do when I feel a little frisky, put on some wooden shoes?

BERTHA. You'll know it when I get you back.

ARLES. You didn't even try to have a good time. You wouldn't even get out of the room.

BERTHA. I counted three rattlesnakes in the parking lot.

ARLES. We have rattlesnakes in Tuna.

BERTHA. Those are our rattlesnakes; they're used to us. I saw one by the porch when we came in. Lord, I hope Jody remembered to lock the back door after he fed Hop-Sing. What a flat tire of a vacation.

ARLES. Don't blame me. I wanted to rent a car and go see that big dam.

BERTHA. I've seen a dam and a lake before.

ARLES. Where?

BERTHA. Lubbock.

ARLES. Oh well, we've been to Lubbock; there's nothing left to do but just lay down and die.

(He finishes off his drink and pours another one.)

ARLES. And we had to leave early. How could we stay if you wouldn't get near the bed? Happy Valentine's Day.

*(Pause, **ARLES** dumps out his drink.)*

BERTHA. I was afraid the bed would come back on again.

ARLES. Baby, you heard the noise that vibrating bed made when it shorted out, it sounded like a milk cow choking on a soccer ball. There's only one thing in the world that could come back after making that kind of sound.

BERTHA. What?

ARLES. Cher.

*(They both laugh. **ARLES** gets punch from fridge and pours a glass.)*

ARLES. You want some punch?

BERTHA. Yes, I'll have some punch. Well, I'm glad we're home. I was so tired of everybody being nice to us.

ARLES. Me too. I don't know what got into 'em.

BERTHA. Aunt Pearl meant well, but I have trouble sleeping with a borrowed cake pan in the house. I don't want to owe someone for an Elvis wedding.

ARLES. Oh, I'd rather eat boiled gravel with dirt gravy.

BERTHA. Don't remind me of that buffet. I guess I just got homesick for Tuna.

ARLES. That's hard to do when the whole town's just down the hall.

BERTHA. Oh God, Arles, there's a snake under the couch!

*(**ARLES** jumps up on to the sofa.)*

ARLES. God almighty, call the sheriff! Where's Petey Fisk?

BERTHA. I told you I'd get you back.

ARLES. Well, I'm so glad that's out of the way. *(sitting)* Okay, we're even. Come sit down here beside me.

BERTHA. Well, I guess we should just chalk up Las Vegas to experience, but I still think we could have saved some time and gotten that fortune teller to help us out. I wasn't really going to believe her. I just wanted to experience something new and fun and to do it with you.

ARLES. Well, baby. Tell you what, you look in the Lubbock paper in the want-ad section. They got a bunch of fortunetellers in there, so you pick one and I'll drive you over there and we'll see what they have to say.

BERTHA. Really? You'll pay for a full session?

ARLES. And after we'll go to that Mexican place on the wrong side of town and get some enchiladas.

BERTHA. I know just the lady. *(She sits beside **ARLES.**)* I hoped this whole idea was going to be a real picker-upper, but when I laid eyes on that tattooed bridesmaid, I knew we were in trouble. I don't think Bob Hope could have made her laugh. Lord, she was sulky.

ARLES. And itchy.

BERTHA. You noticed that, too. I wasn't about to walk down the aisle with a bridesmaid scratching like a bird dog.

ARLES. Well, you've done it.

BERTHA. What?

ARLES. All that talk about itching and scratching and I get this place. *(He indicates his back.)* Get it for me, would you?

BERTHA. Oh.

(She scratches his back.)

ARLES. Lower.

(She scratches lower.)

A little to the left.

(She scratches to the left.)

All right. Now pop the clutch.

(She scratches vigorously.)

Ahhhhhhh! If I could get you to talk dirty when you do that, we'd have the best marriage in Texas.

BERTHA. *(She playfully slaps him.)* We already do.

ARLES. Oh, thank you baby.

BERTHA. Can you tell me something? Why did we feel the need to spend all that money to go someplace to be alone together? We can do that right here. I mean we don't have a big fountain that dances to movie music. But, remember that winter when Buford Posey ran over the water main and it all froze over? Joe Bob brought all the cast of Christmas Carol, and they all sang Winter Wonderland. Las Vegas doesn't have anything like that.

ARLES. And not likely to anytime soon. And you know all that talk about the bright lights out there? They don't hold nothing to the night that lightning hit Cooter Wooten's windmill forty two times in twenty-eight minutes.

BERTHA. Yeah. Melted that metal rooster up on top.

ARLES. Sure as hell did. Remember how she wandered the streets mumbling, "I'm a sinner. God fried my chicken."

BERTHA. And she still has that tick?

ARLES. Oh, she goes off like a coo-coo clock when it rains.

BERTHA. And if we are ever going to renew our vows, I want to do it in our own church, right here in Tuna.

ARLES. With Reverend Sominex?

BERTHA. Be nice. Reverend Merkel is a fine young preacher and he's bound to get better with time.

ARLES. He's fine by me. Hadn't woke me up once.

BERTHA. I oughta slap you.

ARLES. You're so full of promises.

BERTHA. You know I only saw one church in Las Vegas, and it was catty-cornered to Hooters. That is the last thing I want to see after Sunday services, a big sign that says "Hooters."

ARLES. That might inspire some impure thoughts and speaking of which, I'm still bent out of gear we never got you in that swimsuit.

BERTHA. I know. I was looking forward to sitting by the pool with you and maybe even getting in, but I just know I can't do that around anyone I know. I blame my mama. She was so Baptist. She always made me wear a swimsuit that was so loose, I made bubbles ever time I got in the water. Embarrassed me to death.

ARLES. Is that why you never went off the diving board?

BERTHA. Oh, I'd never have done that. Mama wouldn't have it. She said it almost looked like dancing.

ARLES. You need to get some professional help with that "Mama" stuff. Mine messed me up too.

BERTHA. How so?

ARLES. Well, you knew my mama wrote the Bible.

BERTHA. Stop it.

ARLES. She did. She'd pray over anything. It was nothing to walk into the kitchen, and there'd be Mama praying and laying hands on a broken coffee percolator.

BERTHA. Did it work?

ARLES. No, Daddy would fix the short later, and nobody would tell her.

BERTHA. Your mama was nice.

ARLES. Nice, my foot. She nicknamed me Runt. Told the neighbors I was too little to matter much. That's why I played high school football. I'd climb into a big old pile of bodies and grab some old boy by the lips and try to pull them off his head, and I thought about Mama the whole damn time.

BERTHA. People talk about Texas men, but it's really the Texas women who do the real damage.

ARLES. Oh, hell yes.

BERTHA. Well, Arles, I did some thinking on that long plane ride home and I made some decisions about Mama and about us, and I've decided I'm going to quit being afraid and worrying about Mama or the neighbors or the TV preachers and to enjoy life like I've got a right to, and I don't have to run off to Las Vegas to do it.

ARLES. What are you driving at?

(**BERTHA** *goes to the window and pulls the curtains tight.*)

BERTHA. Now don't interrupt me 'til I'm finished. First of all, tonight… (*She pauses.*) Well, tonight… (*She pauses.*) Well, tonight, I want you to leave the lights on.

(*pause*)

ARLES. You mean, when we…Oh, baby!

BERTHA. I'm not finished. I've got something else to show you. Well…about that swimsuit.

(**BERTHA**, *who is now downstage near center, turns her back to the audience and opens up her robe to* **ARLES**.)

Happy Valentine's Day.

ARLES. (*whistles*) Oh, baby, baby, baby.

(**BERTHA** *re-fastens the robe.*)

BERTHA. Well, come on. Get up and help me.

ARLES. Get up? Why?

BERTHA. I need some help with this plastic sheet.

(**BERTHA** *takes out the tarp from the suitcase and hands it to* **ARLES**. *He spreads it on the floor.* **BERTHA** *takes out the water pistol from the suitcase.*)

Squirt squirt.

(**BERTHA** *hands* **ARLES** *the squirt gun and stands down centerstage facing upstage and opens her robe.*)

Not the hair.

(**ARLES** *squirts her.*)

Not there, not there, not there. Oh, that's cold!

(**ARLES** *moves about squirting her from different angles.*)

Arles, stop that. You're like a bad kid.

(**BERTHA** *chases* **ARLES** *off, letting her robe slip down at the last moment and revealing her swimsuit. They exit as party music comes up.*)

The End

**Also by
Jaston Williams, Joe Sears,
and Ed Howard...**

Greater Tuna

A Tuna Christmas

Red, White and Tuna